CARGO

Woody Starkweather

CARGO

CONTENTS

PROLOGUE

The Rector of the Science Institute and his subordinate the Prorector sit patiently at the large table in the meeting room. On the walls, black and white drawings of famous Russian scientists are arranged in a row that begins at the entrance door and proceeds at precise intervals of ten centimeters between each picture around the room until they end at the dirty and broken double casement windows. The windows are covered by curtains, which hide most of the grime even though they are ripped in a few places.

The Prorector glances briefly at his boss, who seems to be staring off into space, then looks up at the row of drawings. He has seen them many times, but he reads again each caption telling of the birth, major exploits, discoveries, and deaths of the great scientists. There is nothing new he can learn from reading them, but there is nothing else to do while waiting for the head of the Physics Department to join them.

He looks at the table itself. It was at one time beautiful in the solid, square way that only oak can provide. It was the kind of artistic style that the old Soviet Union demanded, banishing sentiment and championing order and submission to authority, reflecting the serious purpose of the Science Institute. Now many dings and scratches mar its surface, particularly around the thick edges where sweaty hands have gripped it, fearing retribution for some unanticipated political failing. Other hands have gripped it in anger. He remembers the many partial payments of salary, reduced by 70 or even 80 per cent — robbed really — to pay for paper supplies, new blackboards to replace the cheap Chinese ones that wore out in a year, or a new layer of linoleum in the hallway. Stolen from the general university budget which has been shriveled by the quiet dipping of many greedy administrative fingers, withdrawing a hundred rubles here, a thousand rubles there to pay for a television set that worked, or a kitchen stove with a temperature control. The Prorector recalls that his fingers too have dipped into this pot, but he justifies his action because his salary has diminished slowly over the years — and not only diminished but often paid three months late, fueling the fires of anger. It is a wonder the table has not broken from the anger that has gripped it.

His thoughts expand to include the corruption and bureaucratic delay that have seeped into every institution. He sees an image of rancid sewer water seeping into a lake.

The professors were so hard-pressed for cash they had no choice, or so they reasoned, but to ask the students to pay them for their grades. Soon this evolved into a clear system — so much money to the professor for an A, a little less for a B, and so on. If you pay nothing, you fail. Now even the diplomas must be purchased. No one knows if the students have actually learned anything at the university, so that prospective employers must examine each potential employee to see if they can do the job they are being hired for. And of course the employers also have their hands out. No one gets a job without paying for it with their first month's salary.

Gradually, the Prorector imagines, the value of every service and every product falls into a soft swamp of corruption, and the entire economy slogs through it, more and more slowly, until it comes to a halt — a rusted hulk of ancient machinery buried in muck. The images of filth and decay are beginning to upset the Prorector's digestion, and he tries to find something less fetid to dwell on. His knees press upward against the oak table.

Like the Soviet system itself, the table still stands in the same place, performs the function it has always performed, despite the worn surface and the shabby look. If the Prorector had been able to crawl under the table, which at this moment he thinks would be a relief from boredom, he would find that two of the eight legs are loose in their joints and can be kicked away. He doesn't need to crawl under the table. His feet have encountered these wobbly legs on previous occasions. The loose legs too seem symbolic. Many things are on the verge of collapse. But inertia, and nothing but inertia, keeps the system going.

The Rector glances at his watch. "He is late," he says, stiffening his lips with simmering annoyance.

"He is probably dealing with a crisis," the Prorector says. He cannot keep his cynicism to himself. The system is so moribund that only crises demand attention. The ordinary details of running the university are ignored.

"Perhaps he is working hard to schedule the semester's courses," the Rector says, raising one eyebrow and giving the Prorector a cold look. But the Prorector's cynicism cannot be withered so easily. The semester has already begun, yet in most departments the schedules are only just beginning to appear. In the next few weeks, they will be revised over and over as mistakes and conflicts are discovered and resolved. Every semester begins in this chaos, and everyone accepts it. No one remembers if it was ever done differently.

The Prorector thinks the Rector is an insufferable prig, and he knows the Rector does not like him either. Nevertheless they drink vodka every Saturday afternoon in the Rector's office until they can barely find their way out of the building. But the Prorector knows they do not drink together out of camaraderie. They drink, like most Russians, to numb themselves to the pain of life, and since they dislike each other, each is partly the source of the other's pain, so it makes perverse sense that they should drink together to anesthetize their collaboration.

Finally, the head of the Physics Department comes in out of breath, carrying six worn folders under his arm. He plops the folders on the table carelessly so that they spill and fan out across the table. The Rector's face shows disapproval at the disorder.

"Have Tea?" the Rector asks, his voice weary as he picks up and rings a small bell without waiting for an answer. The head of the Physics Department nods in agreement, and the Prorector smirks. He knows that the Rector himself wants tea, making the offer an empty one. The tinkling brings in the department secretary, who bobs her head quickly and turns to leave before the Rector has finished making his request. He stares at her backside, which is flat and unappealing.

They sit in silence for a while, waiting for the tea.

"Things are well in your department?" the Rector asks in a toneless voice.

"Yes, Sergei Ivanovich. *Kakee dela*, Things go as they go." He uses the nearly untranslatable phrase that gives no information.

"Good," the Rector says. The Prorector notices the Rector has interpreted the answer on the positive side of neutral and smiles wanly.

The tea arrives, an ornate samovar and small glasses in silver holders, and the worker pours a glass for each of the three men, her face without expression. She sets a small bowl of sugar cubes and a pitcher of milk on the table. She is an older woman, wearing dark, conservative clothing, her hair pulled back in a bun. The Rector requested a younger girl that he could at least have ogled from time to time, but the ministry took the younger, attractive ones for its own ogling and sent the dregs on to the various departments. Often the departments found the "dregs" were hard-working and talented, while the ministry has sometimes to pay for its ogling with workers who lack experience or intelligence. Here, as elsewhere, a pretty girl gets some mileage out of her looks so that the pretty ones tend to be less skilled than their plainer counterparts.

They all fill their glasses and sip the tea through sugar cubes held in their mouths in the true Russian way. Then the Rector gets down to business.

"Vladimir Petrovich, we need to discuss Golutsov," he says.

The department head sighs. Golutsov is an albatross that has hung around his neck for many years.

"What has he done now?"

"He has embarrassed the university yet again by introducing his companion, his *imaginary* companion I should say, to a visiting American scientist from the University of Iowa."

Vladimir Petrovich screws up his face in pain and shakes his head as if trying to deny the fact that one of his professors is bizarre, if not downright insane.

"He is crazy, of course," the Head replies as he takes off his glasses and cleans them on his stained necktie.

"Of course. He has always been crazy. Up to now, however, he has done no harm, and his understanding of nuclear weapons is brilliant, so we have continued to find him useful. Now, however, with this latest debacle and the embarrassing explanation to the American, we have decided that he is no longer useful to the university."

"You are firing him?" The department head's face lights up. In contrast to the drab surroundings, his smile is a beam of sunlight coming through the window.

"Yes, we are. The ministry has approved."

"Thank you, Sergei Ivanovich. *Bolshoi s'pacebo*, thank you very much." The Head's enthusiasm for the rare, almost unheard of, action cannot be contained.

"*Vam s'pacebo*— thank *you*," the Rector replies, "for your patience over the years."

It is a nice thing to say, and uncharacteristic, but all three of the men know what a burden Golutsov was to the Physics Department. Even the Prorector finds himself smiling and shaking hands with the department head. The next step of celebration should be a little vodka, but of course they have agreed to fire someone, and it would not be appropriate, so they raise their glasses of tea in the air and look each at the other, one at a time, in a silent but sober toast.

"I will prepare the papers," says the Prorector.

"Well," says the department head, shaking his head. "Well, well."

When he is told, Golutsov is furious, but there is nothing he can do. The ministry has approved the action. There is no union, no ombudsman, no possibility of appeal to a higher authority. He has been fired. *It would not have happened under Stalin*, he thinks. He packs up his top-secret files on nuclear weaponry and leaves, taking his imaginary colleague by the hand and muttering to her about what vengeance he can take.

1. KIMMIE AND TOM

Thursday, 7 a.m. Greenwich Village, New York

I don't usually wear make-up. It seems like hiding the truth — a betrayal of my profession as a journalist. I've been a reporter for close to 15 years, since I was 22, working for major newspapers. Now I'm at the New York Times, the world's leading newspaper (in my humble opinion), and I take my work seriously. This morning, however, I make a tiny exception with lipstick and eyeliner because I'm meeting Tom Shipman, an FBI agent assigned to Manhattan; a guy I've worked with before. Tom's good-looking in the craggy, middle-aged, slightly paunchy way I seem to like lately. When I check the mirror on the way out, I see my summer tan has faded, and the lipstick makes me look even paler, so I take a little off with my finger and dab it on each cheek. It's better. No Dracula look.

Tom's standing in the doorway of a little bagel place in Greenwich Village, near where I used to live. The Village, formerly artsy and countercultural, is now boutiquey and profit-purposeful. We'd agreed to meet there, but I thought he'd be waiting inside.

"It's too cold," I say as I fake-push him backward into the restaurant.

"Hi, Kimmie. Yeah, two minutes and I'd have found us a table. Hey, you look good. Did you change your hair?"

"No. Same old curly blonde. It's all real though. Color, curls, and everything else."

"Well, real's hard to find these days."

"Ain't that the truth," I say in a wise-ass way, and my heart beats a little faster.

During these flirty preliminaries, we get inside, find a table by the window, and sit.

"So," I say, getting down to business. "Is there something real you want to tell me about?" I raise my eyebrows to make the question sound suggestive.

"There is."

A waitress comes over. I need coffee. Tom orders a modest breakfast.

He waits for her to leave then leans forward. "First, the director wanted me to thank you for the work you did on the president's two most recent undersecretary appointees. Your investigative skills were very useful."

"Glad to help. I know how understaffed you are."

"Right. This one's quite different."

"I'm listening."

"There's a sleeper cell — terrorists — in Manhattan," he tells me, as though he's giving me the results of last night's Knicks game. "We think they're trying to smuggle an explosive device into the city. Probably on a container ship. Probably through Elizabeth."

"What kind?" I ask, wondering about the ship.

"We don't know that, but we're worried."

"Meaning?"

"Actually, the director isn't worried at all. He thinks the cell has been dumped."

"Like abandoned by their handlers?"

"Yes. I met with the director just a few days ago, and he reminded me that there has been no communication between them and the new leaders for months. And this particular cell seems to be amateurish. They were trained many years ago. But I don't agree with him. They've been in touch with each other, and those internal emails have picked up in frequency. It all looks innocent to him, but I'm not so sure."

"OK. So what makes you think they're trying to smuggle explosives?"

"It's just a quality in the words they use. Something's changed. They seem a little edgy to me."

"Maybe they *have* been dumped," I suggest. "That would make them nervous."

"Yeah, maybe, but there's something else."

I wait a few seconds, but my eyebrows are starting to get tired of looking as if something was going to happen.

"What?" I ask finally.

"There have been some strange things from Russia — some kind of shake-up in one of the universities, involving one of their nuclear experts. I pointed it out to the director, but he reminded me that the professor that's involved in it is very unreliable, a little crazy in fact. Still, it has me worried."

"Why?"

"I can't help but wonder if they're thinking about bringing in a nuclear device."

"Shit!" I expected him to say something about the ship. A nuclear bomb in New York. It's unthinkable. Like the collapse of the twin towers. I force myself to imagine the devastation — a white-hot blast and radioactive fallout on my favorite city. Then a second image contrasts — the paper running a story, my story, about how the plot was foiled.

I stop that like a bad movie. I'm a reporter. I chase the information wherever it leads me, until I arrive, flushed and out of breath, at the truth. Next to that idealism, ambition seems dirty. But this story's Pulitzer material. Still, I wish I hadn't thought about that.

Tom's appealed to my ambition before. He's appealed to other things too, but he's working an angle now. He's overworked and understaffed, and I can supplement his resources when there's a story in it for me.

He leans forward, and his voice drops even lower. "There's something else too. I got your note that you've moved to the Upper West Side, and two of these guys live in your building, in an apartment right below yours."

"No shit?"

"No. They're right there."

"Should I be worried?"

"No. I just want you to get some more information about these guys. It shouldn't be dangerous. And, you know, it's just a suggestion. You can take it or leave it."

"Suggestion? Are you being suggestive?" I ask, smiling in a way that I'm sure he'll understand.

"Sorry, no. If my suspicions are correct, it *is* serious, and you could help."

"OK. Talk to me."

"I want you to buy some equipment."

He hands me a piece of paper with a list of items that look electronic.

"The bureau will pay for these things. You can have them installed in the guys' apartment and listen in on their conversations."

"Why me? Don't you guys do this for yourselves?"

"Usually, sure. But you live right there now and can monitor their movements as well as listen in. Plus, you've done some investigations for us before."

"But..."

"And it will free up a couple of agents. Right now we're working so many cases — all different kinds — right here in Manhattan. And we tried to get more agents, but the bureau told us to 'be creative' and that's what I'm doing. But there's another reason."

"Yes?"

"People need to know more about these cells. The director doesn't like the bureau to get in the public eye. It always ends up getting political, but having someone like you on it right from the beginning means accurate reporting. You'll know all the details from the beginning. No need for a long series of interviews. And the details will help make sure it's not taken for fake news."

"OK. I get it. Count me in. But fill in the blanks."

Snooping's what I do for a living. Usually I take the high road with Internet research and phone calls to associates, as if digging into dirty laundry is the "high road," but I can get low if I need to.

"It shouldn't be dangerous, but it might take up some of your time." His brows furrow as he realizes that I might say no.

My eyes lock on the cute furrow. "I realize that. But it'd be a great story — worth the time."

"Well, that's your call."

Tom's a straight shooter. When he says something, it's as true as he knows. So I trust him. When we're talking about business, it doesn't matter that I'm a woman. And yet, when it's appropriate, he flirts a little. And he's cute. Not that his looks have anything to do with our arrangement. They're a little something extra, like the mints the hotel maids leave on the pillow.

"Tell me about the guys in the apartment."

"I'll give you whatever we know about this group. And when you write this up for publication, after we're done — whatever that means — I don't need to tell you I can't ever be identified as your source."

I nod.

"The paper would sit on it anyway until it's over," I say, "because of panic."

"Yeah, you're right. People would stampede outta here."

"It'll be our little secret. It's not so little though, is it?"

"No." He pauses. "What about your editor? Doesn't he want to know what you're working on?"

"I'll think of something. I don't think I should tell him. If it came out he knew something big like that beforehand, he'd be in serious trouble."

"And you won't?"

"Well, I might, but that's a risk I'll take."

He looks worried, and his worry warms my heart, but I don't know what to say, and I guess he doesn't either, so we look out the window and watch the passing scene. It's a little before 8 a.m. The early birds are going to work — young business types, mostly female, in their power suits, clutching trench coats against the weather, and a few guys not wearing overcoats, pretending they don't mind the cold. And because it's the Village, there are oddballs — a guy with a long beard, his shirt open down to his waist, with torn jeans and sandals. He looks cold, but he's probably happy wearing the village-the-way-it-used-to-be uniform. Then a guy goes by dressed all in purple — sneakers, jogging suit, ball cap, and riding a purple bicycle.

A woman walks by who doesn't fit any stereotype — middle-aged, in a stylish, maroon cloth coat and excellent heels. She's still good-looking, although she may've gotten a surgical helping hand; her chin looks suspiciously pert. Her blonde hair is curled so it bounces when she walks. That's a masterful touch. At that age, things stop bouncing and begin to droop, so making your hair bounce is fighting back. I'm not there yet, but it isn't far off, so I look for role models.

I jerk my mind back to Tom. Some things I still don't understand.

"Were these guys identified by Homeland Security?"

"No way. That whole thing's just politics."

"Isn't everything?"

"Maybe. Remember that big email trolling operation a few years ago? They identified thousands of 'suspicious' emails, turned them over to us, but all that did was tie up the FBI. They were just innocent people who happened to use the wrong phrases. The real terrorists aren't stupid enough to use those phrases."

"So, how'd the FBI identify these guys?"

"I didn't ask, but I'd guess the usual way — informants, profiling."

"Tell me again why you want this story to come out? After we've nailed them," I add.

"Because the public should know about it."

"You said that before."

"Maybe these guys have been dumped. But there are other terrorists living here too. They could be our neighbors, colleagues, co-workers. They live in our buildings and ride our trains."

He leans forward. "And they want to kill us. People should be more alert, get to know their neighbors. When the public is on the ball, it really helps."

"OK, OK, I get it. I'll give you whatever I find." I pause. "Before it gets in the paper," I add, just to make our arrangement clear. I expect the same from him. There's no point in just pretending we trust each other.

"Yes. Do that. Advance information may give me an edge in catching these guys. But it'll protect you too."

"How?" Up to this point, I'd been thinking that breaking

the law could get me fired. Of course there's the "jail thing," contempt of court for not revealing sources. But, like most reporters, I prefer not to think about that.

"I don't know exactly. I'm thinking you may find out something that's half of something important, and I'll have the other half."

"So, what do I need protection from?"

"These are committed people, whether they've been dumped or not. They're trained, and they won't hesitate to kill you if you're in their way. You read the papers." He smiles. "Hell, you write the papers. Many are eager to commit suicide for their cause. You have to watch out for people like that," he says. I don't smile back; I'm not keen on noir humor — not when it's so close to home anyway. "But all you're going to do is listen in on them. If you're careful, they won't have any idea that you're doing it."

I balance the time it'll take and the small possibility of getting caught by these maybe terrorists against the possibility of a sensational story and reach over the coffee cups to shake his hand. Trying to look into his eyes as I hold his hand, I dunk my sleeve in his coffee. He gives me that killer smile and a handshake that's firm but doesn't crush my rings against my fingers. I'm impressed. He knows exactly how to shake my hand. And he ignores my *faux pas*. While I'm wiping the coffee off my sleeve with a napkin, he goes on.

"Here are three addresses. There are six people — five guys and a woman. They live in pairs. I guess the guy-gal pair is an item, but maybe they're just playing a role."

"And the names they're using?"

He takes out a pen and writes two names after each address. He does this from memory. Then he reaches in his coat pocket and takes out a small envelope. He tilts it toward me and holds the top open so I can see there are photographs inside, pictures of the cell members. He doesn't take the pictures out; he just lets me know they're in the envelope. Then he slides it across the table.

"These are copies. Destroy them as soon as you don't need them," he says, looking steadily at me. "The director would have my ass if these got out too soon."

"OK. We have to preserve your ass. There isn't much of it left." He starts to laugh, but doesn't follow through. Instead he gets up and leaves with just a little wave, not saying anything. He does this — leaves without any parting words. I asked him about it a while back, and he told me a story. He once said goodbye to a colleague after they'd met, and the guy walked out the door and into an ambush which left him dead. It must have been traumatic. I watch him as he walks away. I like his flat little ass. It's even cuter when he's naked. But it's been a few months since I've seen it that way. Hence the flirty stuff.

A woman who starts to make it in a man's world — and newspaper publishing is still a man's world — gives up a lot. Mostly she gives up dates. No one calls. No one flirts. No one even gives you the once-over. I fight this trend, and sometimes I get obvious, but I fight it anyway. That's where all my sexual innuendo comes from. It's how I let the men I talk to know I'm not just one of the guys. And it worked with Tom.

I pay the bill with the money Tom left, tipping the waitress generously so I don't have to pocket the extra. Then I walk out into the wind. Slinging my bag over my head and one shoulder so my arms are free, I walk, clutching my too-thin raincoat with both arms. The wind's cold, and I scurry along, thinking about terrorists, a nuclear bomb, and this wonderful city. It's been over 60 years since the bombs exploded above Hiroshima and Nagasaki. I'm horrified to think the next one might be here.

2. WAZIRISTAN, PAKISTAN

Earlier

Rich tapestries hang from wooden frames set up inside the cave. Rugs from Persia and Turkey cover the floors. Cushions and low tables make an opulent place to have coffee or tea while seated in the Arabic fashion. Here and there are some chairs and tables, because non-Arab visitors also come to speak to the New Leader. Faintly in the background, the sound of Arabic music, its quarter-tone embellishments and ornamentations, can be heard. Incense subtly covers up lingering smells of bat guano and dampness and the sweat of fear, for some visitors do not survive.

The New Leader sits in the soft chair at the head of the table, facing his generals, who have come at his invitation. Thick, sweet coffee has been served, and they all sip it delicately and talk among themselves in low, respectful voices as they wait for the New Leader to speak. He lifts the small coffee cup to his lips delicately, holding the sleeve of his robe aside, then places the cup back in its saucer with careful, almost effeminate, movements. He rises, and with a small wave of his hand, the music stops abruptly. The chatter dies quickly. The generals put their cups down and turn to listen. His speech is soft and gentle with the accent of a cultured, aristocratic Arabic prince.

"I want you to see something," he says, gesturing toward a large screen. They all turn to look. He signals again, and the screen shows a tape of the twin towers in New York City aflame, and then each falling, one after the other. It is a tape made by the Old Leader. In Arabic subtitles it recounts the story of the commercial jets, hijacked by militants and flown into the towers, ending with statistics that describe the damage and devastation and the great loss of life. He wants to remind them of the victory.

After the tape is finished, the men applaud, looking around at each other and smiling. The New Leader rises slowly and expresses his gratitude to Allah for the victory now so many years ago. Then he turns to the generals.

"Yes, it was a great victory, carried out by martyrs of Islam. We were strong then, but today many of our fellow warriors have gone over to ISIS and weakened us." He pauses. "Now ISIS is diminished, and we have an opportunity to increase our number once again."

"But how can we do this, *effendi*?"

"Our warriors deserted us because the voice of ISIS was strong and appealing. So now we must act again and with great strength. We must strike and strike again, at the centers of their financial empire, and we must strike even harder."

"The victory in New York City was a great one, *effendi*, shaking the whole Christian world," says the general.

"Yes, Allah is powerful," says the New Leader, sipping from his cup. "But His power will be seen even more clearly if we can carry out another mission in the same place, a mission that is even more dramatic."

"How can we serve you, *effendi*?" one of the generals asks.

"Let us select some of our trained warriors — those who are already settled in New York, waiting for our signal."

"Yes, of course. There are many there, already trained in many different skills. They have been well taught."

"Select six who have the best English."

"One group has two Americans who trained with us, a man and a woman."

"Even better. They will send a powerful message."

"They have been there for a few years, and as we directed, they have found local employment in sensitive areas — transportation, utilities, etc. — so that they will know best how to circumvent the security systems that have now been strengthened."

"Very well, *effendi*."

"We are going to blow up the city."

The general smiles.

"I see that you believe in this attack."

"Of course, *effendi*."

The general gets up from the table and bows slightly.

"*Insha'Allah*," he says. If Allah wills it.

Months Later

An associate of the New Leader enters from behind a hanging curtain. The New Leader rises from his chair and greets him warmly, shaking his hand and then embracing him. They have worked together on many projects, and now they are performing in a kind of show.

"*As salaam aleikum, effendi*," peace be with you, the newcomer says as they shake hands.

"*Wu aleikum as salaam*," and with your family, replies the New Leader softly but with authority. "Please, be seated."

The newcomer sits down, and a servant immediately serves him coffee and a small plate of sweets, which he accepts with a gracious smile. He waits for the New Leader to begin.

"It is time that we show the infidels once again that Allah is powerful."

"Yes, indeed, *effendi*," the newcomer agrees quickly, "we have waited long enough."

"I have decided that we should bring a nuclear bomb into the very heart of their financial empire, where their new crusade is rooted, as we planned years ago," the New Leader says. It is not a request for agreement, but a statement of fact. "You already have a cell or two in the city, if I am not mistaken," he says, though he knows that such a cell is on station, waiting for the word. In fact, he knows the people's names, the countries they were born in, and the stories of their recruitment and training.

"Yes. They are there, waiting for a signal. There are even two Americans in the group."

The New Leader knows this, but he acts as if the newcomer has brought him important information.

"That will make our message strong. If they are caught or killed, the presence of two Americans in the group will tell the infidels that we have resources they have not considered."

"And the builder of this bomb? Will it be the Russian professor who is a little cracked in the head, or someone else?"

"I think the Russian professor, Golutsov, will do the job well. He is indeed cracked in the head, but in the right way." He smiles. "And for a reasonable fee, he will do as we say."

"Very good. When we spoke last, you had planned to have two of our comrades in the Chechnyan struggle make the offer to him. Is this still your intention?"

"Yes. The Chechens are disciplined and dedicated."

"Good. Who will speak to them?"

"That is the question that remains. It is not an easy task. The Chechens are heavily engaged in their own struggle and may hesitate to help us. I would like to ask two of our Palestinian comrades whom you think may be able to exercise leadership when you and I are gone. If they do this simple job well, we can consider them for something more complex."

"I have two like this. Do you want to see them, or shall I give them the assignment?"

"I would like to see them. I learn about our people from the way they react to me — a certain level of fear is helpful. But they must not lose control. Then they are worthless."

"Very good, *effendi*. I will send them to you. I assume that if they fail, we will no longer need them in the organization."

"That is correct."

Both men know that failure to carry out such an important assignment means instant death.

The newcomer and the New Leader rise and embrace. The New Leader remains standing. The newcomer wants to finish his coffee, but instead he departs quickly.

One Week Later

Escorted by a pair of massive bodyguards, the two visitors enter the area where the New Leader sits. They are originally from Palestine and were tested in that struggle. But this is different. They stop and bow before proceeding. The New Leader beckons to them. His movements are comfortable and graceful, as if he were performing a stately pavane. They notice how slow and controlled he is as they walk forward, feeling uncertain and awkward, like serfs before a master, fearing to look too directly, stumbling, and looking up for reassurance. He beckons again. He is smiling, but the visitors sense that he is impatient.

"*As salaam aleikum, effendi*," they both say in unison, creating more awkwardness. The New Leader sees their anxiety but ignores it and graciously returns the greeting.

"*Wu aleikum as salaam.*"

He asks them to sit with him at the table, and they want to comply, but they are not sure where they should sit until he shows them. And even then, they do not know what to do with their hands.

There are pleasantries — questions about their recent traveling, regrets for the inconvenience of the mountain — but the two visitors brush the regrets aside as nothing compared to the honor of being here. The New Leader also asks about the health of the men's sons and brothers but not of their daughters or sisters. With a quick look and gesture, the New Leader asks for coffee and small plates of candy and cakes. They appear immediately.

The New Leader nods, and one of the servants pours coffee. He gestures for the visitors to help themselves to the sweets. They bob their heads in gratitude and accept the cups with hands that are shaking. They decline to eat.

"Let us attend to business," the New Leader says.

The two visitors nod.

"Our attack on New York City many years ago was very successful." He waits for their replies.

"Oh yes, *effendi*, a great victory." The two visitors smile as they congratulate the New Leader, and he inclines his head slightly to accept the compliment. It had been the Old Leader's idea, but he could accept the compliment anyway.

"Now much time has passed, and we will again show the infidels that Allah is powerful, that God does not love those who do not submit to Him."

"Yes, *effendi*."

"My colleagues and I have considered a number of possibilities. The West is vulnerable in two areas. One is their chemical plants, where highly poisonous gases are stored in large quantities. There is no real security, and it would be easy to set off an explosion that would rupture a tank and send the poisonous gas across a wide area. In the right location, many thousands of people would die."

"This sounds like a good plan, *effendi*, simple to execute and with enormous consequences."

"Yes, it would be easy to do, and perhaps we will pursue it also. But the other possibility is the detonation of an atomic bomb in New York City."

The visitors gasp. Their eyes widen.

"Yes, you see how much more dramatic such a bomb would be. It is always good to kill as many infidels as we can, but our real purpose is to make an impression, to let them know that God is powerful and on our side. So this is the mission we have decided on. I want you to arrange for an atomic bomb to be set off in New York City, as near to the financial center — Wall St. — as possible."

The two men are silent, stroking their beards in thought. It is a bigger idea than either of them has ever had, and they are surprised at the boldness of it. They do not know what to say.

"Yes, I know. It is quite ambitious, but we would not have brought down the towers if we had lacked ambition."

The two men nod.

"It can be done, my brothers, it can be done. The type of bomb that was dropped on Hiroshima to end the Second Great War can be made today, shipped to New York, and driven into the city on a truck. Some of the American newspapers have written about it. They are afraid of it, but they have done nothing to prevent it. They cannot defend themselves against such an attack. The smell of their fear is in my nose."

The two visitors look interested. It would be an enormous feat and bring much honor to them if it could be done. "Tell us what you wish us to do, *effendi*."

"In Chechnya, our comrades struggle daily against the Russian infidels. Still, Russia is where the material for the bomb can be bought. The Chechens are few in number, and their struggle against Russia is fierce. They will need to be convinced to expend time or resources to help us in our struggle. We must convince them with the promise of financial and material aid."

"I see," says one of the two Palestinians. The other nods.

"Here are two names and an email address. These men can help you contact a scientist they know named Golutsov, who can build the bomb. Contact them."

The New Leader hands a slip of paper to one of the visitors. The visitor holds it as if it were a rare species of butterfly. After a pause, he nods briskly.

"We will attend to it, *effendi*."

"You will also need to arrange for the bomb to be transported to a port where it can be loaded onto a container ship bound for a port near New York City. I will arrange for someone to pick up the container and transport it into the city."

"We will do these things."

"Thank you. Now, please help yourself to some of these sweets. They were brought from Germany." The visitors' eyebrows rise. The New Leader is of course very wealthy and can easily import sweets from Europe. They do not notice the irony — if they succeed in destroying the infidels, there will be no more sweets from Europe.

The men take one piece of candy each. They have no interest in sweets at this moment. They are too frightened. They will need to plan these tasks with great care. Suddenly they realize their audience with the New Leader is over, and they rise hastily from their chairs and bow. The New Leader inclines his head, dismissing them.

"You may report to Akhmed," he says, indicating a man standing almost in the shadows. Akhmed comes forward and bows slightly to the two visitors, handing one of them a card, which the visitor studies briefly before tucking it inside his robe.

"Thank you, *effendi*," they say, bowing. "We will accomplish this task."

"*Insha'Allah*," the New Leader says. "If God wills it."

The Next Day

The two Palestinians leave the New Leader's sumptuous underground hideout, riding down the mountain in a jeep summoned from the town below. They do not talk during the ride. Nor do they notice the awe-inspiring mountains around them, snow-covered at the peaks, brown and desolate below, strewn with boulders and stones. Here and there a gnarled tree has sent persistent roots deep into the rocky soil where tiny rivulets of water seep through the karst. It is spring, when the snow above melts and the streams are full.

The stubbornness of these old trees, bent by wind, hardened by season after season of drought and cold, is not unlike the spirit of the people who live in this region. They have known nothing but war and poverty for decades. They no longer hope for peace, and prosperity is a word almost lost from their vocabulary.

Such abstract thoughts are not in the minds of the two men in the jeep. They think of the job they must do — contact two Chechen comrades, fighting for Islam in godless Russia, and convince them of the New Leader's plan. What occupies their minds so intensely is the consequence of failure. They are not close associates of the New Leader. They cannot count on his unswerving support, and most of all they cannot count on his goodwill if their mission should fail. Everyone in the organization knows his mild manner and soft voice belie an uncompromising and ruthless nature. If they fail to recruit the two Chechens, or if the transportation across Russia goes awry, they probably will not survive. If they attract the attention of authorities, or are caught in the act, their death is inevitable, either from the police or from the New Leader himself. He does not tolerate failure and does not want anyone in the organization who cannot carry out an assignment. But if they succeed, they will certainly survive and perhaps be praised. Their success will probably mean other assignments, perhaps more difficult, will be given to them in the future. And then the same set of consequences will present themselves. There is no escape. The only way to exist in such a climate is to recognize that Allah's will prevails. Their job is to submit to it.

When they reach the village in the valley, they hire another car to drive them to the city, several hours away. They stay there for four days while they have false passports and visas and other identification papers prepared. They will travel to Uzbekistan, where they will meet the two Chechens and explain the assignment. It may not be easy to convince the two freedom fighters to make the arrangements the New Leader asks for, but they will do what they can and hopefully, *insha'Allah*, the Chechens will agree to their part, and the two Palestinians will be able to report back to the New Leader that the plan has gone forward.

But first they have to contact the Chechens, and this can be done only by email. So they go to an Internet café and write to the Chechens, using the English language and terms that are nonspecific and businesslike.

> *TO: freechech@mail.ru*
> *SUB: Instructions*
> *Hello brothers,*
> *We met recently with the CEO, who tells usyou have access to markets in your area. Can you meet with us in Uzbekistan to discuss arrangements?*
> *Sincerely,*
> *Yassir ibn Sinai*
> *Muhammad al Tikriti*

They sign the email with the new names they have chosen for their false papers.

The email userid "freechech," however, contains a sequence of letters — "chech" — which triggers an electronic filter in a monitoring system in Europe. At the same time, the last name chosen by one of the Palestinians — al Tikriti — triggers another filter in the United States. Both filters perform the same action — they send the emails to a file, where they are stored until they can be read by an analyst. The analyst will decide whether any of the several hundred emails he reads each day are harmless or not. If he judges them to be harmless, he will save them to another file. If he judges them to be dangerous — indicating an attack or the planning of an attack — he will forward them to his immediate superior, who will make a further determination of action or inaction. Often it is an increase in the volume of such emails that raises the alarm.

In Paris, Jean Sabatier, employed by the *Sûreté* to monitor emails that have been flagged in this way, is drinking strong coffee and smoking while he reads the messages spotted by the system and accumulated during the night. He has spent the night with his mistress and is a little tired. *She was a vixen*, he thinks, smiling at the memories of the previous night. He sees the word "freechech" with the sequence "chech" highlighted in the email address of the respondent.

He reads the email but finds nothing in the content that seems threatening. A flurry of similar messages to the same address might have caught his attention, but there is only this one. If he had been razor-sharp this morning, he would have consulted his list of hot words that the Americans look for and found the name "al Tikriti" on the list, or he might have simply realized Tikrit was the city Saddam Hussein had called hometown. That additional piece of information might have made him decide to send the email on to his boss. But he is not razor-sharp this morning, and the two pieces of information do not come together in his mind.

3. RESEARCH

Thursday, Late Morning. New York

Back in my office, I open the envelope and look at the piece of paper Tom gave me at breakfast: six names next to three addresses. My coffee grows cold, but I sip at it anyway because it might help me think. Two of them living in one of the apartments have the same surname — Yusef and Hussein Al Aksa. That's a made-up name, at least the Al Aksa part, based on the Al Aksa brigades. Another two guys sharing an apartment are Saudi or Kuwaiti or something — Muhammad al Riyadhi and Al Akhbar, the Powerful One; no first name except that his American acquaintances will call him Al. I think he must be a real hot dog, full of himself, to use that name. The last couple, a boy-girl pair, is a real surprise — Rebecca and Nathaniel Jordan. American sounding, or is Jordan a way of Americanizing an Arabic background? But Rebecca and Nathaniel? They sound like a couple from the '50s, playing bridge with the neighbors in sleepytown. They're the ones that live right underneath me.

Looking at the pictures, and the names that go with the faces, I realize I must get the "bugging" equipment, or whatever it's officially called, that Tom listed for me; that means a call to Gaylord, my oldest friend. This is a job he's well suited for. But his voicemail kicks in; he's off until tonight, and I'll need to call him back. I add that to my to-do list.

"Hi, Kimmie. You look worried. Everything OK?" It's my boss, Jim Langdon.

"I'm OK. Thanks, Jim. Just concentrating on a story."

"What about?"

"Uh, cargo ships."

"Is that interesting?"

"Maybe. When I know a little more, I'll tell you about it."

"OK."

He walks on, and I'm relieved. I'm not ready to talk about it.

I Google container shipping. Wikipedia comes up first with descriptions, pictures, diagrams of containers, and the ships that carry them. From other sites I learn the history and the processes of container shipping. Soon the whole industry forms a coherent picture in my mind, and I start writing up information I'll use later. I hope.

After an hour and a half, I'm ready, so I call Jim and ask for a meeting.

"Come on over," he says, like he's in Staten Island.

I walk the 20 feet to his office. I've come up with a reason for writing a story about container shipping. It wasn't hard, and it's pretty much the truth too — just leave out the nuclear bomb part.

He leans back in his chair with his feet on the desk. His heels pin down a story some other reporter's been working on. Like a lot of editors, he works from hard copy. It's not that he disrespects the work reporters do — he's just a slob.

"Have a seat, Kimmie." He gestures me down and waits until my butt's where it belongs.

"What d'you have?"

"Well, first, most cargo comes into the U.S. in container ships. The containers are a standard size, fitting right onto 18-wheelers or flatbed railcars."

"Hmm," Jim grunts. "Where'd the idea for standardizing come from?"

"A truck driver actually. A guy named Malcolm McLean.

He got bored waiting to unload at a port and realized how much more efficient standardized containers would be. It took a while, many years in fact, and a lot of his own money before the industry decided to adopt his idea. Eventually…"

"What's the hook, Kimmie?" He interrupts me. "This sounds more like a class in methods of modern shipping."

"Right." I swallow hard. When an editor interrupts you, you're going down the wrong track. I continue, thinking fast, dropping my plan to tell him about Keith W. Tantlinger, who developed a method for locking the stacked containers to each other so they'd be stable on a rolling ship at sea.

"The hook is we're not protected from what's in those containers."

"Don't they inspect them?"

"A little. Maybe two percent are inspected at the ports."

"That's nothing. Why so little? Wait, don't tell me. It costs too much."

"It's all about efficiency and volume."

"How much volume?" he asks. I know he likes stats, as long as they're interesting, and I glance at my notes.

"About ten container ships dock at American ports each day. Each one carries as many as 10,000 containers."

"Jesus! That's 100,000 containers a day. And only two percent are inspected?" I hear his voice and know the hook is working. But I have to back off just a little to stay completely truthful.

"The coast guard scans a few of them at sea, for radioactivity mostly, but they can only do a few. Most aren't inspected at all." I pause for a minute, trying to gauge his reaction; I don't pick up anything but mild interest, so I go on with more factoids.

"You've probably seen those huge cranes."

"Yeah."

"Those are for the bigger ships. The smaller ones use a RoRo method."

"RoRo? Like row, row, row your boat?"

"More like yo-yo, but horizontal." I can't help but grin. "It stands for roll on, roll off. The trucks drive onto the ships. The ships have their own cranes. They plunk the containers onto the trucks; a crew straps them down, and the truck is on the highway in a few minutes. Thousands of containers, each 40 feet long and 8 feet high, are unloaded and on the road in a day." I can see he's still interested and is beginning to wonder if the *Times'* readers will be too. "The ships are fast too," I go on. "Twenty-eight miles an hour in good weather, crossing the Atlantic in about four days. Merchandise packed in Europe is in U.S. markets in less than a week."

"And a bomb could get through just as fast," he concludes. I know then I've sold the story.

"Exactly."

"A container bomb instead of a truck bomb," he says, veering slightly off course but away from the nuclear bomb idea, which is good. I don't try to expand his thinking. A container full of explosive fertilizer like a truck bomb would do a lot of damage too. And I need to keep some kind of lid on this story for a while.

I go on. "The Feds have gotten hold of some documents showing that terrorist organizations are trying to recruit men who work on container ships. They've already found one terrorist hiding in a container."

"OK," he says, taking his feet off the desk and letting his chair tilt forward. "It's a story, a good hook to scare people a little. Why don't you find out who in the Homeland Security Department oversees the ports and what they're doing to improve the situation?" He pauses. "If anything."

"Right." I've lost whatever faith I had in the Homeland Security Department already, and my "right" probably sounds — hell, it is — sarcastic. Jim twists his mouth and nods slowly. I take this to mean he has the same opinion about the department. His body language tells me our interview is done, and I jump up and hustle back to my little cubicle, eager to find out who has the job of guarding the ports.

The information is hard to find. It seems buried in political and legal issues — the purview of my good friend Max. I give him a call.

***

"Hello, Kimmie." Max puts his hand out. "How's the reportorial life?" Max always says something like that.

"Not bad. How's the juridical life?" I always say something like that. Can't remember when it started.

"Not bad. What can I do for you?"

"I'm working on a story…"

"Of course you are. When are you not?" He smiles that killer smile that hasn't changed in the 20 years I've known him. Max Josephthal and I go back a long way. He used to be in a little storefront in the Village back when Village rents weren't in the stratosphere. He moved to the Upper 80s ten years ago. I finally followed, but to the west side.

Now in his early seventies, he still looks young, trim, and very nattily dressed. He shaves his head, which probably takes a few years off. I've always liked the way he looks. I like his wife too.

"How's Harriet?" I ask quickly, realizing I've not been much of a friend.

"She's good." His eyes swerve over to the picture on his desk for a few seconds. Then they swing back and look straight at me again. "Tell me about the story you're doing."

"You defended a stowaway a few years back. He was in a container, right?"

Max nods.

"I'm doing a story on container ships and need to know how they're loaded and inspected. I thought you could tell me."

"Ah, you mean Timur Shah, the Uighur refugee. He was an odd fellow, but mistreated by our government. It's hard being a Uighur under Chinese rule. The 'fleeing persecution' was easy enough to document. I just had to convince the jury our government had labeled him a 'terrorist' for political reasons — to stoke fear in advance of the election that year. It wasn't so hard."

"I need to understand how he got into the container. I recall he got out by banging on the container's side once he landed on shore. The look on those longshoremen's faces must have been priceless. What he looked like, how he smelled. I can't imagine surviving four weeks cooped up inside a metal container." I stop myself. I'm going off topic. "I need to know about the inspections; how often they're made, or just how they're made."

"It's far too easy to get in. All it takes is a bribe. That's how Timur did it anyway, in China. But in many countries, too many, it's just that easy."

I've come to the right place. Again. Max never fails to come through.

"You're going to have a hell of a story. I'll put you in touch with someone I've known even longer than I've known you. It'll take a few days though. I'll text you when I can say more."

And with that, our conversation is over.

***

As the elevator doors close, I take out the piece of paper with the addresses Tom gave me and look at it. Seeing my new street address next to one of the names is still a shock, and for a moment, I have to reorient myself.

"Just across the park," I say.

"You can get a cab on Madison," says a guy in the elevator, smiling.

"Did I say that out loud?"

He nods, grinning. I shake my head.

"Too much on my mind." I flash him a big grin like we're old buddies. I can see the grin has an effect, and I feel glad I can still do that. Then the elevator doors open. I give him a little wave as I walk out. I hope he's watching me walk away, but I don't look back.

I walk to Madison and get a cab heading west. As we go through the park, I sit back and look out the window. I love Central Park. It's an oasis of greenery in a gray concrete desert, and it provides a little tranquility. New York's not a calm place, and having an island of serenity means a lot. All hail to the guys who keep it green and flowering.

***

The cab comes out of Central Park five blocks away from my apartment, and it takes a few minutes to pull up in front. I pay the cabbie, adding a good tip. The tip is part of their salary, after all. If they do their job, they get 15 per cent. If they do something extra, I'll give them a little more. If I think they haven't done their job, I give them less. It makes me partly their employer, which is the way it should be. There are a lot of things like that in the city. Things that are the way they should be. Because we're all crowded together, living on top of one another — literally — stepping over and around each other all the time, we develop the social rules; we figure out how to get along maybe a little better than those people who live in the pumpkin patches of America. They don't really have to get along. They can always walk away, go home, sleep in a haystack, whatever. They're almost hermits by comparison to the average city dweller. I marvel at how elaborate my mind can become just by thinking for a minute about my tipping rules. I probably should have been a professor so I could get paid for spinning theories out of gossamer factoids. It works for investigative reporters too.

As I slam the cab door behind me, I need coffee, and there's a perfectly good coffee shop across the street. So, looking both ways first, I dash across. Inside I find a stool where I can look out the window at the entrance to their building. It's "our building," I realize with a shudder.

I order my coffee. The waitress is typical — middle-aged, female, a little broad in the beam, and her uniform a little too tight; someone who's been around the block but stopped off for a doughnut. I'm sure she'll call me "hon" when she puts the coffee cup down, but all I get is a bored look. I guess you have to sit in a booth to get the term of endearment. Maybe she's tired. I sure am.

I look again at the pictures Tom gave me and the six names, hoping one of them will come out so I can follow him to the place where they'll unload the bomb. I crumple that idea up and toss it into the corner with the other dumb ideas. Then I start thinking. These guys must work somewhere or go to school. They must do something during the day except hang around planning massive explosions. I can call directory assistance on my cell phone and get their telephone number. Besides, the coffee's excellent, and it appears I'm getting free refills. So I call. Alphabetically. Al Akhbar's number comes up, and I'm automatically connected. Now why don't they have an unlisted number like everyone else in New York, I wonder? These guys aren't poor, living in this neighborhood. Maybe they want someone to be able to look them up and call them.

"Is this Mr. Akhbar?" I ask with the innocent voice of the telemarketer trying not to get hung up on.

"No. Al's not here. He's at work." There's an accent in the voice, but it's faint. The guy's pronunciation of English — and this must be Muhammad — is pretty good. So much for stereotypes.

"Can you give me that number?" I ask, trying not to push the innocence too far.

"Sure. It's in the phone book under Consolidated Edison." I think I detect some sarcasm at this point, but I could be wrong. Still, terrorists can be sarcastic. If they can be murderous, they can be sarcastic.

"Right. Thanks. Sorry I bothered you," I say, quickly.

I hang up and Google Con Ed then ask for the personnel department.

"Consolidated Edison," says a male voice.

"I'm looking for a Mr. Albert Akhbar." There's a little bit of silence while he looks up something.

"Mr. Akhbar's crew is in the field at this moment. Can I patch you through?"

"Sure. Patch me through."

Two rings then, "This is Al."

"Mr. Akhbar?" I use the same innocent voice.

"Yes." His voice is surly. *Ooh*, I say to myself. *He sounds tough.*

"Mr. Akhbar, do you know every day thousands of people die suddenly without warning and leave their loved ones completely helpless?" I know it isn't very imaginative, but I've already accomplished my purpose. The creative juices have stopped flowing.

He hangs up.

"That's a decisive man," I say, putting my hand over the coffee cup when the waitress returns.

"Well hang on to him, honey. There aren't too many of those left."

"You got that right." I slip off the stool. "And thanks for calling me honey. I was beginning to think I'd forgotten to brush my teeth." She gives me one of those meant-to-be-fake smiles as she turns and bumps the door to the kitchen open with her well-padded butt.

I head home where I can make the rest of these calls with my feet up.

***

How lucky can a girl get? I grab the elevator, and scooting in right behind me are "the Jordans" — Rebecca and Nathaniel. Talk about timing! It's the first time I've seen them in the flesh, and I give them the standard New York smile that's supposed to say "Nice to see you; don't come too close." At least they smile back; same one. I studied the pictures Tom gave me, but pictures tell a skimpy tale. I see how young they are, by my standards, probably under 30, though Rebecca could be older. Somehow, in their short lives, they've come to hate their own country. That's a peculiar thing.

Most people are naturally patriotic, I think. We love the place where we grew up, where our friends and family are, where the scenery looks familiar and the values match our own. Of course, lots of people are critical of the government or their current mayor, but that's like arguments in a healthy family, butting heads over matters of principle. Often, in a family, the arguing comes from the love people feel for each other. It's the same with a country. People who criticize the government want their country to be as good as it can be. But when someone gets so twisted they want to damage their own country and hurt their fellow citizens, something's very wrong. As a reporter, I know there's a story in Rebecca's and Nathaniel's backgrounds, and probably not a pretty one.

Nathaniel's on the short side, about 5'7", and Becca, which is what I hear him call her, is an inch or two taller, making them an improbable couple. He has dark brown, straight hair, parted on one side, and brown eyes that smolder. Women might go for that. His hair tends to fall on his forehead, and he pushes it back with his fingers. He's slender but strong looking, wiry even. His hands, I notice as he pushes the elevator buttons, are small, and he uses them with delicacy. I wonder if he's been an artist of some kind.

Becca has blonde hair that's either natural or very professionally colored. It's that honey-blonde color that in dark light looks brown, but in the sunlight is much lighter and sparkles with gold highlights. I want hair like that, but I don't think I can tell my beautician there's a terrorist with hair I like. Another thing — they both look really fit, like they go to a gym regularly, which implies an optimistic view of the future and maybe good values. Well, maybe not good values.

***

If Al is in Con Ed, what are the other crucial support services in New York? I make a list: transportation, communication, water, waste removal, and money — banking and finance. Somewhere in the middle of those vital city functions, I'll find them. By the end of the day, I've learned a lot.

Becca Jordan works for the subway system as a secretary in their central office. She has access to a lot of information

— personnel, schedules, equipment, track repair, finance, and security.

Nat's employed by the Port of New York Authority, a file clerk in the bridges and tunnels division. I realize I'm already thinking of him as "Nat." I guess we're getting close. He could learn about the Authority's policies and procedures for security of those vital links between New York City and New Jersey, Connecticut, and upstate.

Al's roommate, Muhammad, is working as an office assistant for the FTC — the Federal Trade Commission. That's puzzling. The first three I found were so obviously placed to learn about the city's defenses. Probably he is too, but I can't figure out how. I make a note to ask Tom.

The last two are easy — they're driving a garbage truck. They probably don't have access to critical information, but I figure there's a lot they can do to help plant a bomb. Driving a truck is a useful skill. That's when I realize with a shock if you're going to import a nuclear bomb in a shipping container, you need a truck to get it from the boat to the city. I try not to worry about it.

4. MAKING A BOMB

Petrozavodsk, Russia, Summer

Nicolas Antoninovich Golutsov is a clever and resourceful man without a shred of political or social sensibility. He sees no more value in democracy than in totalitarianism, no less value in communism than in capitalism, no difference between nationalism and globalization. It is all the same to him. He feels, in fact, a little above all these squabbling ideas. He was trained in science, and he has faith in the scientific method and in the scientific way of seeing things. He likes to say, "Science is the way Europeans see the world." Science, he feels, is not much different than the dream songs of Australian aborigines or the mythical accounts of the Native Americans or African tales of the supernatural. It is no truer than these different world views, nor is it better, simply different. However, Nico, as he likes to be called, thinks himself a European, so he believes his view is correct — he believes in science. But he recognizes that the aborigine painting dream songs on didgeridoos in the outback of Australia also believes in his particular world-view. Thinking like this allows Nico to see himself as more tolerant and understanding of other people, who may not share his level of technological education. And so, in the end, he feels superior to most other people, whether of his own cultural persuasion or of another. In other words, below the surface he is an arrogant bastard.

He is not married. The idea of living with a woman and a passel of children does not appeal to him. It seems messy, in a way, and he abhors messiness. So he relieves his sexual needs by himself — in a way.

He never knew his parents. He was left by his mother at an orphanage, where, along with 120 other children in like circumstances, he was housed, fed, and clothed but not in the least nurtured; a childhood that made it easy for him to wall off some aspects of his thoughts from others. His early life also helped him enjoy, even crave, solitude. And yet, the times alone were long, and as a child he learned to create imaginary friends.

Although he has no wife, he does have an odd habit for a grown man — he has an imaginary "playmate," actually more of an imaginary colleague, but since his work is for him a kind of play, it comes to the same thing. As he works in his laboratory and workshop, he talks to Nina, as he calls her, or Ninochka when he feels affectionate. Nina and Nico work together, but they are also friends. She is usually present when Nico takes a break for tea, and she often listens to him discuss the work he's doing — should he include such-and-such a device? Nina will suggest the answer. "The formula for calculating explosive force is what? Oh, yes, thank you Nina; I forgot." He talks to her like this during most of the workday. And when he needs sexual relief, Nina is always ready to remove her lab coat and lean back against the workbench, arching her back and moaning in ecstasy. She really is the perfect colleague.

His sense of superiority and his belief that he is above political differences mean he does not have to overcome any nationalistic or cultural scruples when he enters his workshop in the basement of the house on Nagueskaya St., in the city of Petrozavodsk, where he is assembling a small nuclear bomb. A leading terrorist, once an associate of Bin Laden himself, now hiding in a cave in Pakistan, asked him to do so. The inquiry came to him some time ago via two Chechens, who told him he could make a great deal of money, $6 million in fact, if he put such a device together. Half of the money was given to him up front, and much of it was used to obtain the necessary materials, particularly the enriched uranium, which was expensive. The Chechens said he would get the other half once the device was detonated in New York City. He could pick up his money personally from the New Leader in Waziristan.

He checked the whole deal out with Nina, and she approved of it enthusiastically, and what better confirmation than the approval of his closest friend, lover, and lab partner?

Nothing in this arrangement seems out of joint with the way the modern world works, as far as Golutsov can tell. There's an active black market in weapons, and enriched uranium is a substance that can be purchased. He even knew, from his former colleagues at the Physics Department of the University of Petrozavodsk, where a quantity of uranium of sufficient size and quality could be bought. It was simply expensive.

His arrogance was heated to the point of anger when the university fired him. He is brilliant, and he knows it, but his colleagues find him difficult to associate with. At a party given to honor a visiting American scientist, he forgot himself for a moment and introduced Nina to the honoree. Usually he is careful about such things, remembering when he needs to that Nina is imaginary, but the American's casual manner and easygoing nature had befuddled him just a little, and he had slipped. When the American realized Golutsov was trying to introduce him to an imaginary person, he politely and adroitly removed himself from the conversation and then mentioned it to the department head. It was not the first time Golutsov had embarrassed the department; his file had a list of such incidents stretching over most of his career. In disgust, the head went to the ministry with yet another complaint about the physicist. A few weeks later, the ministry approved his termination of employment, to the relief of many.

The Chechens came to him later with their $6 million offer. He accepted the offer quickly, but he had to think hard about the technology. The Chechens said the bomb would be transported from Petrozavodsk to St. Petersburg by truck, and then from St. Petersburg to New York by container ship. If he simply built a replica of the Little Boy bomb that was dropped on Hiroshima, it would weigh 9,000 pounds, and that would make transportation quite difficult, so he had to figure out a way to make it much lighter. He and Nina explored the science together. The original Little Boy was heavy because of the steel jacket that enclosed the "gun barrel."

The device itself is simple — a barrel of metal with two masses of uranium-235 (enriched) at either end. A relatively small explosion at one end shoots one of the masses down the barrel like a bullet. When it collides with the other mass, it begins a chain reaction in which some of the atoms of the uranium break apart, releasing a large amount of energy. This explosion causes more of the uranium in the now combined masses to collide with itself and thus break apart more atoms which increases the explosion, creating the well-described chain reaction. The longer the explosion is contained within the casing, the more fission occurs. Every millisecond before the casing bursts enhances the effect; but once the explosion rips the casing apart, the chain reaction stops. So the enormous weight of the ironically named Little Boy came from the thickness of the steel casing, which served two purposes — to contain the small conventional explosion that fired the bullet, and to contain the chain reaction for a few milliseconds so that it could grow.

Golutsov has an idea about the weight problem. Materials science has progressed since the days of Los Alamos, and today there are ceramics as strong as steel but much lighter. Nina thinks he can construct a ceramic "hull" around the basic barrel of steel that will contain the initial stages of the chain reaction. The barrel itself can still be made of steel, but it can be thin, and he can make it work even better by shaping the conventional explosive charge that drives the "bullet" down the barrel. They didn't have shaped charges at Los Alamos. The ceramic hull will be very strong but light.

He imagines two ceramic casings separated from each other and from the steel barrel by many small struts, each strut at an angle and braced against its neighbor. The resistance will be enormous. Golutsov and Nina calculate the resistance in kilos per square centimeter. When the two hulls are combined, each with its substrate of catted struts, the resistance is a little better than the original design, and the bomb will weigh much less. On paper, it seems doable, but he will need to do some tests, particularly regarding the ceramic component.

He uses some of his seed money to help the local ceramics factory beef up its capacity so the half-hulls and the little struts can be molded and fired in a superheated furnace, and he searches for, and finds, the materials for the new ceramics, which contain a couple of catalyst substances in addition to the usual silicas. He carefully measures and writes up his specifications. The ceramics people are very eager for his business because it improves their capacity. With the addition of the superheating kiln, they will be able to manufacture household knives and other new-age ceramic products that will be greeted enthusiastically by the growing market throughout Russia. Eventually those former Soviet Republics, still struggling to establish their economies without the help of Mother Russia, will expand this market. The future of the factory looks brighter because of Golutsov's business. Golutsov supervises the modifications of the new kiln.

When it is upgraded, he is the first customer, having submitted his detailed specifications months earlier. The testing begins.

The hulls are not exactly right at first. The new technology requires new formulas for the shrinking that firing produces, and the factory must discover those for itself, because information of this sort is not readily shared among the growing businesses of the new Russia. Quite the contrary, theft and espionage among rival companies are the norm, and the company hires additional security personnel to make sure their discovery of the shrinkage formulas are not stolen by their rivals.

After several modifications and additional testing, the factory develops a ceramic that is up to the task. They cast the hull pieces and deliver them to Golutsov. But he performs some additional tests and modifies the formulas further. Eventually the factory makes a casting that is exactly right, and Golutsov carries his first two half-hulls and a large supply of struts home with him in his little Lada automobile. The half-hulls are so light he can carry each of them in one hand. The plastic bag of struts swings from one of his hands. This good casting of the inner hull and the struts weighs a little more than 20 pounds. The thin steel barrel will be the heaviest part of the device.

Back in his lab, he painstakingly epoxies each of the struts to the steel barrel, measuring the angle and the height of each one. There is some tolerance for error because the epoxy, which is also very strong, fills in any empty spaces. But he is careful and does not need to rely on the epoxy's space-occupying characteristic more than a few times. When the steel barrel is covered with four rows of struts on each side, he checks for the fit of the hull by chalking each strut's tip and then pressing the half-hull against it. All the chalk marks transfer to the inside of the half-hull so he knows exactly where to put the dabs of epoxy. When all of this is done, he presses the half-hull into position and clamps it in place. The next day he repeats the process with the other half-hull and cements the two half-hulls together with epoxy. These seams will be the weakest part of the construction, but he thinks they will not be very weak.

When the first hull is assembled, he orders a new supply of struts and attaches them to the outside of the inner hull. Then he submits the specifications for the outer hull to the factory, and they turn out the two half-hulls even faster, and more accurately, than with the inner hulls. They are a little heavier than the inner hulls, being larger, and he makes two trips from the factory to his Lada, but they are still amazingly light. Then he begins the process of fastening the outer hull to the struts already in place on the inner hull.

***

Golutsov enters his lab the following morning and sees with pleasure that the double-hulled casing is complete. Nina smiles beside his accomplishment. He is excited at his success and makes love to Nina on the spot. She also enjoys his success and shows it in a number of ways that have never occurred to Golutsov.

When he's "relaxed," he approaches the task of packing the larger portion of uranium into the receiving end of the barrel. He puts on a lead-lined helmet, lead-lined coveralls, and protective gloves before removing the uranium from its lead canister. He packs the radioactive material into a steel container he has made that fits exactly inside the barrel. He spreads epoxy on one end of the container. Then he latches the container to a long-handled tamping tool he has made for the purpose and pushes the fissionable material all the way into the barrel until it contacts the steel barrier at the end. He is amused at how similar this process is to loading an old-fashioned musket.

When he feels the end of the metal container contact the rear barrier, he pushes a little harder and twists the tamping tool for a better epoxy joint. Then he releases the tamper from its latches and withdraws it.

The last part of the assembly is the firing charge that will send the "bullet" down the barrel, ramming it into the other mass of fissionable material. The firing charge fits like a cap over the other end of the bomb barrel. It has three parts — the detonator, the conventional charge, and the second batch of uranium — which must be assembled in order and placed in the firing charge cap before the whole cap can be attached to the bomb. The detonator is equipped with electrical contacts so that it can be triggered by a timer. The force of the explosion will be so huge that the person placing the bomb will need considerable time to get away. After the detonator is inserted into the cap, the conventional explosive is placed next to it. Golutsov moves with great care and precision as he places the explosive up against the detonator. An accident at this time would not generate an atomic explosion, but it would kill him just the same. He sweats a lot and pauses several times to wait for his hands to stop shaking before he can proceed. Finally, the detonator and conventional explosive are in place. Then he inserts the "bullet" of uranium. There is less danger of an accident in this process, and he works with greater ease. The assembled firing cap is quite heavy. A substantial wall of steel lies behind the detonator so it can withstand completely the force of the conventional explosive. Otherwise the bullet would be sent down the barrel with less than maximum force. It does not, however, have to be strong enough to withstand a nuclear explosion because at the time of the chain reaction at the other end of the barrel, the fissionable material in the bullet will also be exploding and countering the force of the fissionable material with which it has come into contact. The cap will of course be blown off in the nuclear explosion but only after a few milliseconds, all it takes to reach the maximum force of the chain reaction.

Once the cap is assembled, he attaches it with epoxy to the two hulls. Then he attaches a timer to the cap and equips it with a receiver so it can be set remotely to count down a specific amount of time, and a "trigger" that can initiate the countdown.

With a sense of accomplishment big enough to fit his overinflated ego, he puts these finishing touches on the bomb then lifts its 500 pounds with a chain hoist, slips the crate frame he has made under it, and lowers it in. Once in the crate, the scientific work is done, and he and Nina celebrate with a bottle of champagne bought for the purpose.

The crate is a little too large for the entryway to his workshop, and he enlarges the opening to get the bomb out. Then he sends a coded message to the Chechens that the device is ready to be picked up. They in turn send a message to the Palestinians, who make arrangements for a shipping container already destined for New York to be partially unpacked and reloaded with the bomb inside the legitimate load.

The money Golutsov will get from this project is substantial. He will put it into a foreign account, Switzerland most likely, then obtain a travel visa for the U.S. Once there, he thinks he will spend several years improving his English, and then decide — either to live in some comfort but not real wealth off the earnings of the $3 million he will have left, or perhaps to teach in the Physics Department of a Midwestern university. The Midwest has always appealed to him. Nina will like it too, he knows. She came from peasant stock and likes uncomplicated things. He thinks of the Midwest as a simple, uncomplicated place, filled with farmers who raise crops and sell them to the government.

He also imagines life is easy and uncomplicated in Iowa or Minnesota. He does not think the people in these places care very much about politics or know very much about the outside world. He is wrong on both counts. Nevertheless, his yearning for a life of comfort and simplicity is the ironic basis for his bomb-building.

He is not at all troubled by the consequences of his activities. He figures once he completes his job and hands the bomb over to the two Chechens, his responsibilities are over. What they choose to do with the bomb is entirely their business. He knows they are going to ship it to New York and detonate it in the middle of the city, but he takes no responsibility for the lives that will be lost when this is done. He is merely a businessman. It is not personal. Making money has a morality of its own, separate from ordinary morality. Within the world of the businessman, he is simply using his skills to make and sell a product. It does not seem important to him that the people who enforce and administer the law, both in his current and in his future country, see things very differently. In this, he simply deludes himself. Nina agrees with him completely about the morality of his enterprise, and that helps relieve any traces of guilt he might feel about making the bomb.

When the two Chechens appear at his door to pick up his "product," he greets them with politeness and takes them into the basement workshop, where the bomb is caged in its wooden crate. The double doors leading up to street level have been removed from the frames, and the frames themselves have been taken from the walls. This allows a clearance of a little less than an inch on either side. There is no possibility of turning, but no turning is needed. The crate simply must be carried up the stairs. The outer doors at the top of the stairs swing out and are attached to the wall with strap hinges. The pivots of these hinges protrude into the opening only one-half inch on the two sides, leaving enough clearance for the crate to pass.

The three of them try to lift the crate, and they can get it off the ground, but they need more help to get it up the stairs and into the panel truck waiting outside. The two Chechens leave to get help and return in less than half an hour with three helpers, hired off the street. It is always easy to find strong young men eager to help in the muscle work of any project. There are not many jobs in "Petro," as the young people call the town.

With the additional help, the bomb is loaded into the panel truck and driven away. Nico closes the outer doors and reattaches the doorframe at the bottom of the stairs then rehangs the door itself. When he is done, he claps his hands together to announce the completion of the project, makes love to Nina, pressing her lissome body against the workshop wall, and then goes upstairs to pack for his trip to Pakistan.

The flight from Petro to Moscow is short and uneventful. He waits for two hours in the airport, intensely aware of the seediness of the airport facilities. Then he boards a plane for Peshawar. This flight is boring and quite long. Only one Russian language newspaper is offered, and he reads it twice from cover to cover. He knows his fellow travelers would not understand his bringing Nina along; she is on another flight.

The cacophony of the Peshawar airport assaults his ears. Grimacing, he makes his way through Customs and Immigration. His papers are all in order, but he emerges in a bad temper anyway and is greeted by an unsmiling Pakistani man, dressed in the Arabic fashion, holding in front of his chest a sign with Golutsov's name on it. The man does not speak Russian, and neither of them knows very much English, so he follows gestures that invite him to accompany the Arab to a small car, put his suitcase in the trunk, and climb into the passenger seat. He is tired from the journey and falls asleep during the early part of what proves to be a nine-hour trip. Toward the end, when Nico is fully awake, they climb mountain roads that twist unmercifully and are strewn with loose rocks and rubble. The going is both rough and unpredictable, and Nico is nervous. The driver is not reckless, but the road is so difficult any driver would find it hard to navigate. Nina, who is in the back seat, is smart enough to keep quiet.

Finally they arrive with relief at the entrance to the cave, where the driver lets him off and retrieves his suitcase from the trunk. Inside the cave he is taken down a side passage to a room, superbly furnished and decorated like a fine hotel. In English laced with occasional Russian and German words, servants tell him he has three hours to rest before meeting with his benefactor, the man who commissioned him to build the "*Malchik*," or Little Boy.

He is delighted to find Nina is waiting there for him in his room.

5. KIMMIE AND GAYLORD

Gaylord's probably the smartest person I know. He owns a store called Twisted Wires, and he's a wizard when it comes to anything electronic. He also stands out as totally outrageous in a city where outrageous makes people yawn.

Gaylord grew up in the projects in the Bronx with his mother and four brothers. When he was 12, he realized he liked to dress up in women's clothes and concluded he must be gay. He made a tactical error and came out to his whole family one night while they were eating Colonel Sanders and watching reruns. His mother cried. His brothers attacked and pummeled him so hard he ran out of the house. He went to the home of a gay man he knew and moved in.

That relationship didn't work out very well, it seems, because whenever we come to that part of Gaylord's life, he stops talking, and there's very little that can make Gaylord stop talking. It turned out he wasn't gay. He just liked playing roles, including female ones.

It's hard to describe Gaylord because he likes to pretend he's different types of people, and he's always changing his appearance. One day he'll be dressed like a street punk in faded jeans, felony shoes, and a hoodie. The next day he'll have on low riders and a bare midriff that shows his washboard abs, falsies, and a wig, looking like a sexy teenybopper. And he pulls it off, although he likes to leave some little sign that makes it clear he's male. Hair on his chest maybe, or a cigarette pack rolled in the sleeve of his tee shirt (he doesn't smoke). He always uses the name Gaylord, however, which he took on when he was 12. He still enjoys the humor of it. I don't know his real name. No one does, and he won't tell. New York is full of quirky characters, which is one reason I love it so much.

Twisted Wires is in the East Village, and I take the train downtown, changing at Columbus Circle. When the Village became trendy and expensive, the genuine Village people couldn't afford it anymore, and the East Village is where they went. It's arty and funky, the way the Village used to be. I pull my coat tighter as I cross the square. The morning's nippy, and the wind blows scraps of paper and dead leaves until they pile up in brown and white drifts against the gray buildings. In the East Village, people are just waking up, trying to find the instant coffee through a fog of sleepiness.

Gaylord has obviously been up for hours getting presentable. He's in drag, dressed as a kind of Deanna Durban type with plucked eyebrows, slicked-down short hair, crimson lipstick, and an orange turban. He has on a bright orange, slinky silk dress, with a deeply delving neckline, and yellow stiletto heels. If he bends down, you can see the edges of his falsies. He's shaved the hair on his chest, which I'm grateful for. Sometimes Gaylord wears a dark business suit and wingtips and shakes my hand with a serious face. But not today. Today he's dressed like a '30s diva and acting the part. I look him over, trying to discover the telltale sign he always leaves about his masculinity. I finally find it. There's a bulge at his crotch that would have scared Ms. Durban out of her turban. Once I see it, I'm surprised I didn't notice it first thing. I find the whole ensemble, including the codpiece, if that's what it is, very sexy and am surprised at myself.

I'm wearing jeans and a black tee that says "Save the Males" in honor of Gaylord. I feel way underdressed.

"Kimmie sweetie!" he warbles as soon as I walk in the door. He swoops down on me like a mother eagle and brackets my face with two air kisses that are almost a foot away from my cheeks. His hands are on my shoulders, and I notice he's wearing large, yellow-beaded bracelets that clatter. They match his shoes. I think about the white running shoes I'm wearing. They match the lettering on my tee shirt.

"What brings you to my little shop of horrors?"

"I need your advice. Love the turban." I realize belatedly I'm supposed to comment on the packaging.

"Thank you, oh thank you." His voice soars up into stratospheric levels, and he pats his hand against the side of his turban. "Advice, huh? Well, little blonde thing, anything I have is yours, anything at all. Trouble with a man?" He leans back with his hands on my shoulders and looks down his nose in a parody of sisterly suspicion. "Or a woman?" His tone overflows with dribbles of sexual innuendo. He looks me up and down. "Your little pussy fits right in those jeans doesn't it?" He leers.

"No, nothing so interesting." I try not to blush and steer the topic away from parts of my body I keep out of public discussion.

"I'm going to spy on some people, and I need some equipment." I keep my voice low.

"No problem, sweet thing. You've come to the right place. Tell Gaylord all about it. Landline, cell phone, computer, or in the house?" He pauses and the leer comes back. "In the bedroom perhaps?"

"What's the difference?"

"You're talking about M-O-N-E-Y, aren't you?" Now he's being coy.

"That too." I hand him the list Tom gave me, and he takes a long look at it.

"Well, monitoring their cell phone is the easiest. I have the device your friend listed. It'll pick up every call within a certain radius, and the radius is adjustable."

"That sounds very helpful. How much? I'll have to give an accounting to the guy I'm working with."

"For you, because of the cornflower blue of your eyes, $135. You'll hear all calls within the radius. The program displays the number of the caller you're listening to, and once you find your party," he smiles briefly then returns to business, "you can restrict your listening to that number."

"Sounds great. What about the other three devices — to monitor the landlines, their computer, and inside the apartment itself?"

"For the apartment and the landline, little blue eyes," he looks right into them so the blush starts again, "you have to sneak in and plant something. You have to penetrate the enemy's defenses and leave a little something behind, like Don Juan." He wiggles his hips suggestively.

"I get the idea. And how much will this little broadcasting spermatozoon cost?"

"Cheap, very cheap. $75 each, but you have to do the installation."

"I'll take it, although I don't know how I'm going to get it in there."

"I may be able to help you with that too." He has a conspiratorial tone at this point.

"Gaylord, you're a man…" I pause, questioning with my eyebrows, until he nods grudgingly, "of many…" I pause again, this time purely for effect, and glance down at his crotch, "of many parts," I say. I'm beginning to enjoy this game.

"Ooh, sweetness, for that you get a discount. I'll come to your place tonight with the details."

"I've moved to the Upper West Side."

"You whaaaat?" He drags the syllable out and lets his voice go back up into orbit. "You're a Village person, through and through."

"I know, I know. But this apartment is working for me." In more ways than one, I think.

"Well in that case, give me the address."

"What about the computer?" I say as I hand him my new business card.

"Do you know the party's email address?"

"There are parties. I'll get them to you."

"Good. Once we do the installation, you can send a little email that will, so to speak, report back to you. Or, if you like, I can easily slip a little device into the computer that'll send you a copy of every keystroke — only $75," he adds, anticipating my next question.

"These things don't cost very much."

"Tell me about it. There's hardly any money in spying anymore." A little bell signals someone has come in the front door. "Well, I have other customers, I see."

"I'll see you tonight," I say as I slip two $100 bills into Gaylord's outstretched hand.

He glances down and smiles. "I'll bring it all." Then he looks down at the address on the card and shakes his head in silent wonder at the idea of me on the Upper West Side. I wave as I head for the door.

"No wait. Tonight's Friday. It'll have to be first thing in the morning," he says. I just nod.

**

It begins to rain as I walk back to the office. And it's a cold rain, typical at this time of year. I grab a bus. The New York City buses are a great bargain. Sure, they take you where you want to go, but you can also look out the window and see the people. New Yorkers in the rain are funny. They hold newspapers over their heads. I've never seen that anywhere else. In New York a newspaper's not just something to read; it's a temporary umbrella the local environment provides, like the big leaves Robinson Crusoe used on his deserted island.

New Yorkers also try to jump across puddles instead of walking around them. Sometimes they make it to the other side. Passing buses splash pedestrians with the careless abandon of huge dinosaurs stepping on mice in the jungle. New Yorkers know when they hear bus tires hitting water, they swing the umbrella down toward the sound because the bus splashes more water than the rain, and dirty water too.

I regret getting off the warm bus, but step bravely over a puddle and run from the bus stop a half block to the building. It's raining hard, and inside I have to shake my head to get the water off, like a big blonde poodle. My hair is short but curly, so it holds a lot of water. Shaking gets most of it out and splatters the floor and walls. A few swift dabs from a paper towel and I'm almost presentable.

I think again about these six people. Two are Americans; are the others Islamic fundamentalists? Even though homegrown white males make far more terror attacks, Islamic fundamentalists are seen as the world's bad boys. The whole issue is a puzzle. Setting off bombs and killing innocent people doesn't make a group popular, and it doesn't make money; in fact it costs a lot. They aren't trying to convert people or get rich. I sit and think about it for a while, but my silent analysis doesn't get me any real information, just clarifies my opinions, and I can't report opinions. The important things now are the practicalities. How are they going to get a bomb here; a bomb that'll explode with tremendous force if it's jostled too hard.

I don't know, and I don't like not knowing.

***

I turn off my computer, push my chair back a little, and stare at the darkened screen. On my desk are names, addresses, and pictures of six terrorists living in Manhattan, information I got from Tom. I've added the employers but the Googling told me nothing about the method they're going to use, or their timing.

I know the fissionable material, left over from the Cold War, is for sale, as is the expertise. There are many people in the world, and some of them are angry, or insane, or intent on destroying Western civilization. I'm often amazed at the number of people who are certifiable goony birds, to use the technical terminology.

I think back to September 11, 2001, when two planes smashed into the World Trade Center, and the heat brought down both towers, shocking the world. I try to imagine the terrorists' minds, but the level of anger, insanity, ambition, or twisted belief they must have had is difficult to comprehend.

Of course, I remind myself, it isn't the first time men have reached such depths of destruction. From the religious excesses of a millennium ago, when knights crusaded into the Holy Land to destroy "infidels," to the more modern "troubles" of Ireland, the Holocaust, the slave trade, and many, many wars, it's evident people will be as murderous as technology permits. And when they use their religion, or warped versions of it, for legitimacy, it's an emotional accelerant. I don't blame the religions; it's the people who use religion to fit their own misshapen ideas who are responsible.

When the towers fell, I was working in Chicago. I remember the early gasps and cries of "Oh my God," and then the hush

65

that came over the newsroom as we realized how many people were being buried in the falling concrete, steel, and glass. Then a phone rang. Then another. Reporters began calling friends and relatives in New York. The noise level in the newsroom went from a funereal silence to ear-blistering cacophony in a few minutes as we turned to our jobs of getting the story into words and on paper. And then, for the rest of the day, stories kept coming in — clouds of dust, acts of heroism, the president sitting befuddled in a classroom full of children, not knowing what to do. One story after another, and each one only adding to the horror. We learned about the plane that flew into the Pentagon, and hours later, of the in-flight heroism of a few who saved another target but lost their lives in a field in Pennsylvania.

In the decades since, many reporters have tried to get inside the mind of those who'd wrought such destruction. And many thought they had them figured out. I've never been sure.

6. THE PRISONER

A Cave in Waziristan

"Bring him to me," the New Leader says as he gathers his robes around him and sits down with slow dignity, preparing to wait.

"Yes, *effendi*," his obese subaltern answers before turning to exit the ornately decorated room.

No one speaks. The other two men also sit, off to one side, waiting with their New Leader. Softly, in the background, the sound of ancient Arabic music plays, with the quarter tones sliding into the ear and jabbing at the melody. Behind the music is the distant whir of the generator that lights the lavishly furnished underground dwelling. It is opulent, but it might just as well be a prison because the white-robed New Leader, to whom everyone makes obeisance, cannot leave without risking death from a laser-guided rocket.

From time to time, he walks to the entrance of the cave. From there, with the roof still over his head, he can look out over the valley, but he cannot leave. The drones flying unseen high overhead can see him, can even identify him, and within minutes they can launch deadly force, targeted on his person. There would be a blinding flash, and someone else, already chosen and prepared, would have to take over the leadership of the world's terrorists.

So he sits quietly, with the patience Allah (blessed be He) has given him, and for which he is justly famous, waiting for the visitor to be brought in. The fat man comes in and walks up to the New Leader.

"He is here, *effendi*," the fat man says, bowing his head

slightly and gesturing toward the door with one hand while the other clutches his robes.

"Show him in."

The guard opens the door, and the fat man nods. Professor Golutsov, wearing Western clothes, enters slowly, one step at a time, looking from left to right at the rich tapestries hanging on the walls, the deeply cushioned furniture set on the thick Persian rugs. It is a scene from *One Thousand and One Nights*.

Across the room sits the New Leader, beckoning at Golutsov, who hesitates and swallows. The New Leader has great power, and if he wants, he can have the man shot or beheaded by merely looking at one of his colleagues and making the appropriate gesture. Instead he beckons again, and Golutsov approaches, not speaking.

"Tell me the news," the New Leader says.

"The ' *Malchik*' has been sent, *effendi*," says Golutsov. The New Leader realizes someone has coached Golutsov in the proper term of respect.

"And when will the Little Boy do his mischief?" the New Leader asks.

"The ship will stop at Rotterdam to take on additional cargo, which will require a day or two. After that it will be four days before it reaches New Jersey, and perhaps one more day before it is on Manhattan Island, *insha'Allah*," he says, invoking the traditional Muslim prayer for a wished-for future event. Arabic is not his language, and he mispronounces the phrase slightly, but the New Leader overlooks it. He thinks instead that Golutsov is trying to ingratiate himself by using this common Muslim phrase.

"*Insha'Allah*," echoes the New Leader. "You have done well, my friend. We have wished to send this mischievous Little Boy to the heart of America — the financial heart — for many years.

You have earned a great reward."

Golutsov's eyes brighten.

"And you shall receive it when the city is destroyed," the New Leader adds.

"Yes, *effendi*," Golutsov says. He wants to argue that he has completed his part of the job and should be paid, but he senses in the New Leader's quiet self-assurance that it would not be wise to argue with him.

"Meanwhile, you shall be our guest." He claps his hands, and a door behind him opens. A servant enters, carrying a low table which he places in front of the Russian. Another is set in front of the New Leader. A second servant and then a third also appear, carrying trays with small urns of coffee, and plates of dainty food, sweets, cakes, and small pieces of meat. A white cloth is laid across Golutsov's lap.

He shudders slightly. Being a "guest" means he is held prisoner. If the bomb goes off successfully, he will receive his second half. Probably he will leave the stony trails and sandy wastes of these lands and travel to his romantic Minnesota. But if something goes wrong, if the plan fails, he will die. Golutsov has lost control, and his life is in the balance. The New Leader, watching him, suspects he is aware of his situation. Golutsov tries to eat the food, but he cannot swallow easily, and his hands tremble as he lifts the coffee cup.

The New Leader smiles a little. He enjoys having the power to make men tremble. Sometimes when he signals that they are to be executed, their bowels loosen, and they soil themselves. He enjoys that too. Having control over other men's bowels is a distinct pleasure, unlike any other.

He raises his coffee cup to his lips and looks over the rim at Golutsov. It is too bad he must use these Western men. Even if they are Muslim, they are not true believers. And this man is not even a Muslim. He would rather have only the purest of true believers working for him, but he can find none who have the knowledge to make this Little Boy do his bidding. He decides then that when this operation is over, regardless of the outcome, he will have the man killed. It will save a considerable sum. He smiles again. It pleases him to be entertaining a man who has already been sentenced to die.

Golutsov sees the little smiles, and his body relaxes with misguided relief.

7. INSTALLATION

Saturday, Early Morning. New York

I'm waiting at my window for Gaylord and his friend, watching the clouds darken as they threaten a chilly rain. I watch the scene below on 81st St. New Yorkers don't walk like people in Kansas or Iowa where they walk as if walking were pleasant, which it can be. In New York people walk with purpose. No walking for pleasure here. Of course people do walk for pleasure in New York, but they don't want people to think so. It would mean you had nothing to do. That's a no-no in New York. We're human doings not human beings. You can see something in the swing of New Yorkers' arms and the way they carry their head straight up, shoulders back a little — long quick strides. They have a goal — maybe business or maybe not, but something serious. But the stride is often fake. They have no more purpose than the folks in Iowa. It's just that New York is all about image. Anyone sauntering on West 81st St. is either up to no good or a tourist. No New Yorker wants to be taken for a tourist.

People are wearing jackets and topcoats, though winter's still two months away. Winter in New York is unpleasant except for the first snowfall, which is fabulous, covering the city with a rare beauty. After that it's all slush, ice, nasty wind, and short tempers. Thank God for the theater and the concerts.

I see Gaylord come around the corner. He looks quite normal today — jeans, leather jacket over a white tee that peeks out at the neck, a black watch cap, and neon sneakers. Well, almost normal — the sneakers are a bit much. His friend is a little shorter, white, and from the window he looks awfully young, walking along with his hands in his khaki pockets and wearing a Mets cap *and* a Mets jacket. It's cool in NYC to wear a Mets cap or a Mets jacket, but wearing both marks you immediately as not knowing when to stop, which is one of the important social clues. You're therefore a nerd. Yes, this guy coming with Gaylord is probably a nerd; no social graces but techno smart.

Just then, Becca and Nat leave the building together, gym bags in hand. Gaylord and friend could get a real close-up, but of course they don't know Becca and Nat from my Aunt Sally and Uncle Bo.

The bell rings, and I buzz them in with a simple, "Hey."

"The coast is clear," I say as soon as they're at the door. "They just left."

"Convenient." Gaylord steps inside. "We won't have to come back on Monday. What's the number?"

"3B."

His nerdy little friend says nothing. Gaylord gets down to business. He's a different person when he's not in his store. Of course that's not saying very much. Gaylord's a different person every day.

We all troop out into the hallway. I wait for Gaylord to introduce me to his pal, but he doesn't, and I guess the omission is intentional. The guy probably doesn't want me to know who he is. We are, after all, about to engage in illegal entry.

We go down one flight in the elevator and walk along the hallway to 3B. The little friend pulls what looks like a small Allen wrench out of his khakis and opens the lock in about three seconds. He still hasn't said a word. There's a second lock, which also yields quickly. Then, finally, he speaks.

"No police lock. That would have been hard."

It would have been impossible, I think. A police lock is a

heavy steel bar that braces one end on the floor and the other up against a bracket on the door and is locked in place there. They're supposed to be impregnable, and I can't imagine how anyone could get past one.

The door opens, making a little noise — a click and a creak. It scares me for a moment. For all we know, there's a large, bearded terrorist with a machine gun waiting inside, or a booby-trap bomb set to explode when the door opens. But there's no boom, and nerdy teen goes in to reconnoiter. We wait in the hall, and I worry about a neighbor seeing us. When he comes back, he's noticeably less tense. We go in, and he closes the door behind us.

I look around. There are four rooms laid out just like my apartment. The kitchen's the first thing you see, but I'm not interested in it, so I walk toward the back. Gaylord and friend have gone ahead of me. There are two bedrooms, and I look in both. One has a made bed, pajamas on a chair, and slippers tossed nearby. The other has a rumpled, unmade bed and a single pillow with a deep impression in it from what I know must be Nat's head. They're not a couple. Or, if they are, they're having a major fight. The third room's an office, with a computer at a workstation, a separate desk with neatly arranged stacks of papers, and a small bookshelf. It looks too neat to be Nat's stuff. I examine the top papers without touching them. Bills, correspondence, some pamphlets on health, nothing at all incriminating. The books are mostly fiction, but there's some nonfiction — on body-building and fitness – obviously a shared interest. Out of the corner of my eye, I see Gaylord's friend screwing a cover plate back over an electrical outlet. He's planted the bug already.

Gaylord comes over and looks at the computer. He pulls the CPU forward so he can look behind it, finds what he's looking for, and presses something into the back. When he leans back, I can't even see it. He's plugged the device into a port on the back but left it looking like the port it was, just a little bigger. Maybe an expert could spot it.

We're done in less than five minutes and head for the door. If this were a B movie, the couple would come back, having forgotten something, and surprise us, but this is real life. The nerdy guy makes sure the doors are locked the way we found them, and we head back to my apartment.

As soon as we're inside, everyone breathes.

"Thanks," I say to the nerdy guy and include Gaylord with a glance. The nerd allows a tiny smile.

"Let's see if it works." Gaylord is being practical.

He fishes the receiver out of the bag he brought, puts it on the window sill, and turns it on. We can hear the traffic noises coming through it.

"It's working," he says. "You'll want to set it on voice activation so you don't record all the traffic." He shows me the buttons to push then goes to my computer and turns it on.

"Would you get the thumb drive?"

I find it in the bag and hand it to him then watch as he slips it in and loads the software. This takes a little time. Then he runs the program. On the screen a notice appears: "Remote computer off."

"It'll go automatically to this program when they turn it on, and it'll send you a record of everything he does on the computer and every email that comes in. Got it?"

"Got it." I say this with more certainty than I feel.

"Call me if something isn't right."

"Thanks."

"Now for the cell-phone receiver." I'm glad he remembers because I'd forgotten about it. He fishes out the little box, opens it up, and plugs it into the wall then shows me where to put batteries if I want to use it outside. He turns it on, and I hear a lot of voices. We tune in one after the other as he shows me how to alter the frequencies.

"The targets are at work now, right?" He looks up at me from the little box.

"Probably the gym. Or on their way."

"When you know they're in the neighborhood but outside, like one of them is shopping, and the other one calls to say pick up more toilet paper, you'll be able to identify the frequency they use. It may take a while to find the right frequency. But once you have it, you can stay tuned to their phone, and you'll hear everything they say."

"I should be able to hear the cell phone ring on the bug we just planted, shouldn't I? If it's in the apartment?" I think maybe this would be a good way to identify them.

"Yes, you should, but you'll have to turn the voice activation feature off. I always knew you were a smart girl." Some of that twinkle comes back into his eyes. "When you hear a cell phone ring on the bug listener and you can hear what they're saying, tune around on the cell-phone listener frequencies until you get the same conversation. Then you can set the listener to that frequency, and you'll be able to listen in on their cell-phone calls. Then you can turn the voice activation back on."

"Is there any chance they'll know someone was in their apartment?" I'm still a little worried about this.

The little friend suddenly pipes up. "Yes. It's possible. I checked for the usual tags — hairs across the doorsill, etc., but I didn't see anything. But it's not difficult to leave something very small that's disturbed by the air movements we make walking around."

I look at him carefully for the first time. He's had a lot of experience doing this kind of thing, and he looks to be 14 years old. Well, maybe 16, or even 18. It's hard for me to tell anymore. But still. There must be a lot of bugging going on, I think. It sounds like a song title to me — "There's a Whole Lot of Bugging Going On." And I have an urge to giggle.

It's suddenly very quiet.

This is the spy business, and it feels like it'll be fun. Of course, Gaylord makes things feel that way, even though he's been uncharacteristically businesslike today.

Gaylord smiles, and his whole face changes. It's like the sun coming out after an afternoon of clouds. He's really a cute guy. A bit young for me, though, like maybe 20 years too young. I remind myself I'm seeing Tom these days.

I smile a thank you at the nerdy guy as they're leaving. I'll never know who he is.

Then it gets quiet. All my devices, except the cell-phone listener, are turned on, but there's nothing. Well, of course. They're not home.

It's time to call Tom. There's so much to tell him.

***

"Tom Shipman," he says, answering his phone, and I can hear in his voice he's not having a good day. Who would, working on a Saturday? Then I realize I've always done that. My job is my life. It's only 9:45 a.m., but at the FBI a lot of bad things could have happened already.

"It's Kimmie. You sound terrible."

"Yeah. Terrible's not bad as a description of how I feel."

"How come?"

"It's the same thing. What we talked about." His voice is guarded, deep, quieter than usual. I figure there's somebody else in the room with him.

"It sounds like you can't talk very freely."

"Yes, that's right."

"OK. I'll be the quarterback. Well, I got some tidbits for you — nothing meaty though."

"OK."

"Three of them work for the city, two in garbage collection, one for the trains. A fourth works for Con Ed, a fifth for the Port Authority, Bridges and Tunnels. All obviously good choices. The sixth for the FTC. I can't figure that last one out; it doesn't fit."

"I'm afraid it does." I can hear the seriousness in his voice.

"Why? What?" I'm lost and babbling.

"That's where a person can find out about the computer systems that are used at the stock markets, both the New York Stock Exchange and AMEX. A person who understands those computers could mess up the system, which would throw us back into the financial dark ages."

"I see," realizing, and disturbed by, how much control these six people could exert over our lives.

"What d'you figure they can do with that information?" he asks, but I know he knows the answer. He just doesn't want to say it out loud.

"If they know how the security system works, they can figure out how to bypass it, or damage it, penetrate the weak points." I'm saying the obvious. "The same goes for the market's computer system."

"Right, that's exactly right. You got it." I catch on. He wants me to keep going in the same direction.

"OK, and I live one floor above two of them. The other four live in two apartments across the street." I say this just to keep talking. He knows where they live.

"The window-shade signal," he says, jumping over several

conversational hurdles at the same time. Sometimes he's a mental superman, able to leap tall ideas in a single bound.

"Exactly. I have their windows picked out. If something changes, I'll let you know."

"You done good." He tries to sound like a West Virginia hillbilly. He fails, but the effort increases his sex appeal.

"Thanks, but my day job isn't going so well. I need a story I can actually print."

8. THE DIRTY YELLOW CONTAINER

A Cosmetics Factory in Petrozavodsk, Russia

A young man, employed as a driver by the Novokozmetiko Company, has been lucky enough to be designated by the U.S. Government as a Temporary Customs Officer or TCO. It is a new program designed to prevent the importation of dangerous cargo in container ships. His recent assignment is to supervise the loading of 200 cases of cosmetic products, bound for the retail trade in New York City. He is eager to get on with the job because his designation as TCO will provide him with a considerable bonus above his salary from the cosmetics company. He studies the paperwork for his assignment while waiting for the truck to arrive. He sees that the container will be offloaded in Elizabeth, NJ, onto a flatbed that will deliver the load to a distributor in New York City. He looks at his watch. The truck is late, and he sighs at the inevitability of delay. He fills out the manifest that describes the cargo, the name and registration of the ship the container will be loaded on, its scheduled arrival in Elizabeth, and the authorization for the container to be offloaded.

Eventually, the truck arrives at the factory, and two drivers load the cosmetics cartons then call for a cab to take them into the red-light district, where they will spend the night. After they have left, two men the TCO has never seen before approach him. They are darker than the average Russian, and he suspects they are Chechens. Although he is a loyal Russian and therefore suspicious of Chechens, he cannot refuse the offer the Chechens make him — more money than he has ever seen, and much more than his TCO bonus, provided he lets them remove some of the cartons and bury a large crate in the container amid the remaining cartons. What could be the harm? All he has to do is unlock the container, alter the manifest to account for the missing cartons, and relock the container when they are done. The size of the bribe easily overcomes any scruples against assisting Chechens or betraying his U.S. employer. One of his children needs expensive medical care. With the bribe, he can afford to pay for the child's services and still put away a nest egg. As for the U.S. Customs job, he will not need it anymore. He might be investigated, but he doubts that the United States will bother. If they do, he will move to another location and find another job. What could be the risk?

So that night he puts the altered manifest in the truck's glove compartment and waits around until the other employees have gone home. The Chechens come in a small truck with three other men, and he unlocks the container. First they unload most of the cosmetics cartons, leaving a layer across the floor of the container. Then they load a heavy crate on top of this layer, placing it in the middle. He notices they handle it very carefully. The crate is about seven feet long and four feet high and four feet wide. He estimates its weight at over 500 pounds, but the Chechens come with three helpers in another car, and they have no trouble placing it. Once the crate is in place, they pack the previously unloaded cosmetics cartons around it until the container is filled. The crate will not be seen when the back of the container is opened, as they know it will be by Customs officers at the harbor in St. Petersburg, who will examine the manifest and compare it with what they could see of the cargo. Also the cartons of cosmetics protect the contents of the crate from sudden impacts. The helpers leave in their car, and the Chechens load the remaining cartons into their pickup.

The TCO waits on the loading dock and watches as they do this. In the pocket of his jacket is a wad of U.S. dollars that feel so delicious his fingers warm and tingle as they touch and caress them. He smiles to himself as the Chechens work. His work is finished. Maybe he will quit his job. With the money, he can hire someone to smuggle him and his family into America. He could start a new life, an idea that appeals to him more and more. In America he will not have to work on Saturday. In America his pay will arrive on time so he will not have to borrow from his wife's parents.

When they are finished, the Chechens close the container and relock it. The two who had been giving orders walk over to the TCO who is still smiling and caressing the dollars, lost in his thoughts of a new life.

"*S'pacebo*," says the taller of the two men. "Thanks."

"*Vam s'pacebo*," says the TCO. "Thank you." They are very polite.

"*Spakonye noch*," they say, waving. "Good night."

"*Spakonye noch*," he answers and turns to head home. A few seconds later, there is an odd noise, and he crumples to the loading dock. A dark pool of blood spreads from under his head. It runs to the edge of the loading dock and spills over onto the ground beneath. The two Chechens wait for a few minutes until the twitching and trembling stop, then one of them retrieves a heavy plastic body bag from their car. They take the money from the TCO's jacket, pick up his body and place it inside then close the zipper. Being careful not to step in any of the pooled blood, they carry the body to their car, bend it in the middle, and put it in the trunk. They come back and dump a bag of kitty litter over the two pools of blood. They examine the manifest in the glove compartment and write down the routing information and unloading details. Then they drive off, heading for a deserted dock in the harbor area, where, under cover of night, they weight the body down and dump it in the sea. Later they send the information from the manifest to the Al Qaeda men who hired them. He sends the information on to his superiors who send it to the cell in New York City.

The two drivers come in the morning and drive the truck and its container away. They pay no attention to the two patches of kitty litter, now an odd, brown color, one on the loading dock and the other on the ground beneath it. It looks like debris from a previous loading job. They show their identification papers and sign the appropriate documents inside the building then climb aboard the truck and leave. It is not until later in the day that someone realizes the TCO is missing, but three days pass before anyone thinks his disappearance is worth reporting to the company boss, who assumes the man has gone on a bender or run away with a woman.

The TCO's wife misses him immediately but is afraid to call his workplace. She thinks it is possible he has been with another woman for the past few days, and that his colleagues at work would know about it. Talking to them would be humiliating. Eventually, however, the authorities are brought in. They question the employees who knew the man, scrutinize his workstation, and study his job description. When they hear he spends a lot of time on the loading dock, they go outside and look at it. Luckily they notice the small, flat piles of kitty litter among the other loading-dock debris and examine them. They take a small package of it back to the police station, where it is analyzed and identified as blood-soaked kitty litter. It is consequently more than ten days before anyone knows the TCO has met with foul play. His body, encased in plastic and weighted with stones, has drifted toward the riverbed and then moved slowly, appropriately funereal and solemn, with the flow of the river. It is never recovered.

On the Road to St. Petersburg

The two-day trip to St. Petersburg is uneventful. In fact the truckers are bored most of the time and talk about how much fun they had on their one night in St. Petersburg, which made the trip worthwhile.

Their night out was indeed wild, and now, the morning after, they drive slowly and speak carefully, describing with pride the hangovers they nurse, tributes to the glory of the night's drunken escapades.

Ahead they see the ships of the harbor, one of which is their destination. They pull off to the side and wait in a queue of trucks, each carrying shipping containers, in front of a low, cinderblock building. It is a relief to stop the bumping and swerving on the road, which had jostled their hangovers. Twice in the morning, they'd had to stop and throw up on the side of the road.

Two Customs officials spot the truck and its cargo and go to it, even though it is still down the line, ignoring the three trucks in front of it. The drivers do not understand why they are being taken care of ahead of those in front of them and are a little embarrassed to receive the special treatment. They do not know the Chechens who bribed them have also bribed the Customs officers.

As soon as the officers have looked at their papers and opened the back gate of the container, supposedly to verify it is loaded with cartons of cosmetics but really to show to any of their superiors who might be watching from the building that they have indeed inspected the container's cargo, they sign the papers and wave the drivers out of the queue and send them in the direction of the dock. For them, it is effortless money, more substantial than the usual bribe.

There are four large ships tied up at the dock, and the drivers stop and pull over to check their papers, making sure they go to the right one. It is not as large as the other three, but it is a RoRo type. Following the signs, they drive directly onto the ship and up to a large crane that has just finished depositing a blue container on top of a red one. The crane operator has, from his cab, locked it tightly to the containers below it.

The truck pulls up to the marked spot, and the two drivers climb slowly down from the cab, still trying not to jangle their sore brains, to unhook the chains that attach the container to the flatbed trailer. As soon as the chains are undone, two ground crewmen slip the heavy bands from the crane under the container through channels on its lower side, ratchet the bands tight, and signal to the crane operator to hoist away. The container lifts smoothly straight up, well balanced because the heavy crate has been properly placed, and the crane moves it ponderously over the stack.

The drivers climb back into their cab and drive the empty truck away before the container is even lowered. It ends up in the third tier up from the deck, third row from the starboard side, and the fourth cross-array from the bow of the container ship. A crewmember standing on the top of the stack unhooks the lifting bands, and the crane mechanism moves across the stack to the platform where the next truck is already waiting. The crane operator locks the unit's lower corners to the container it rests on. The drivers of the empty flatbed are already on their way home. They don't know, or care, but the container will be inspected again electronically during the voyage.

The St. Petersburg Dock

Captain Alexandr Timurovich Zhakdin looks down from the

bridge of the *Rodina* at the dockyard scene below. He watches with some concern as the ramp used by the RoRo trucks is pulled back from the ship. The workers on the docks are never as careful of his ship as he would like, and he always supervises their efforts very closely. To the other officers and crew of his ship, he refers to the dockworkers as "monkeys." Contempt for those who work on shore is an old tradition in the Russian Merchant Marine. They are only dock monkeys, sissies, "light blue" (Russian slang for gay) guys who lack the courage to go to sea.

Alexei, as his friends call him, is a careful man. He grew up in Kazakhstan, in the town of Issyk, where the only water was in the streams that roared down in the spring from snow-melt on the Tien Shan mountains and then dwindled in the summer to a trickle, forcing the herds of scrawny cattle to pick their way across the rounded stones to drink. Nevertheless, as a boy he sat and watched the streams, fascinated by the way they connected the mountains to the seas and lakes. Often he threw a piece of paper or an empty can into the streams and watched it whirl away, heading toward something unknown but big and important.

It became a dream of his to see the sea. He needed dreams. His father was a Kazakh and his mother a Russian, a combination that meant he did not fit in with either of the two main ethnic groups in the southern part of Kazakhstan. He spent much of his time alone, reading books about the sea and boats, imagining himself looking out over an expanse of blue and white ocean. He studied English assiduously to gain access to the wider world. When he finished high school, he traveled across the vast Kazakh Steppe to Aktau, on the shores of the Caspian Sea, where a series of jobs taught him the basics of working on cargo ships. In time, the Caspian seemed small, and he hitch-hiked across the Caucasus to Istanbul, where he found work on cargo ships that traveled through the Dardanelles and on down to the Mediterranean and out to the Atlantic. The Atlantic was as big and wonderful as he had imagined, and he wanted never to leave it.

He worked hard and earned a reputation as a solid mate. He managed to avoid the intrigues and fights that often broke out among bored crewmembers, and he became a kind of peacemaker, arbitrating the little disputes until tempers cooled off. This above-the-crowd stance helped him rise through the ranks. When he could, he would take time off and attend school in Amsterdam or Le Havre or Oslo where he learned about navigation, the law of the sea, management, and the mechanics of a large cargo vessel. In time he became captain of the *Rodina*, a small container ship with a home port in St. Petersburg and making regular runs to ports in Europe and the U.S. His youthful training as a social outcast in Issyk prepared him well for the loneliness of command, and his main social contacts remained the weekly letters he wrote to family back in Kazakhstan.

Zhakdin is known in the industry as one who attends to details, a careful and exacting captain who searches out a problem and tracks it down single-mindedly to its source and eliminates it. The slightest hint that something was amiss in the containers now stacked and locked to each other like Lego blocks in the hold of his ship would keep him from sailing until he understood the problem. If he knew that one dirty yellow container in the hold held an atomic bomb cradled among cartons of cheap cosmetics like a parasitic cuckoo's egg in the nest of an innocent magpie, he would take extraordinary steps to remove the horror.

But he knows nothing about it. Each container has its

own bill of lading, describing the source, contents, and exact destination of its cargo. In addition, all but a handful of these containers, bound for the United States, are equipped with a new device, allowing him to check with an on-board computer whether the contents of each container match the description on the bill of lading.

After the RoRo ramp is pulled away, he gives the orders to cast off — first the spring lines then the fore and aft docking lines — and signals by radio to the tugboats attending him to begin moving the ship away from the dock. The tugs rev up their engines, tightening the huge hawsers until they are visibly thinner, and the ship moves a few inches to the side, displacing tons of water around the stem and stern, the sideways motion unnatural and awkward for any vessel. He lets out a long breath of relief when the ship is some distance from the dock and able to move through the water in a forward direction. Then the grace of her lines allows the water to slip around her with little turbulence. She is a ship then, not a lump of resistance, even though still pulled, pushed, and maneuvered by tugs.

When the last of the lines connecting the *Rodina* to the tugs have been cast off and she clears the St. Petersburg harbor, when the radio messages of thanks and goodbye have been sent and received, she is at last at sea. Captain Zhakdin sinks gratefully into his chair on the bridge, still watchful, still alert, but at last in tune with the environment around him, the blue and white sea of his youthful dreams.

He rings for the galley.

"*Pazhalsta, chai smolokom,*" he says into the microphone, ordering tea with milk to be brought to the bridge.

"*Kanyeshna, Kapitein, sichass,*" comes the eager-to-please reply.

In less than ten minutes, an orderly arrives on the bridge,

carrying a tray with a small pot of brewed black tea, a larger pot with hot water, a pitcher of milk, and a small bowl of the candies the captain enjoys eating with his afternoon tea. The surfaces of the tea and milk shimmer with concentric ripples from the engines' vibrations. The vibrations are low now in both frequency and amplitude, but as soon as the ship is well clear of the harbor approaches, the vibrations will increase, and they will not diminish until the ship reaches the outskirts of its next port of call.

The Dutch Port of Rotterdam

The Dutch port of Rotterdam is a modern, efficient operation. As the *Rodina* approaches the harbor, a pilot boat comes out to meet her, and a qualified pilot comes aboard to bring the ship in. Captain Zhakdin remains on the bridge during the piloting, which includes the taking on of lines from tugboats that will pull the *Rodina* to its assigned dock. Some captains retire to their cabins during piloting to do the paperwork necessary in dropping off and taking on containers, but Zhakdin is not one of them. Should there be a mishap of some kind, he wants to be present.

But there are no mishaps. Had there been even one, the ancient port city of Rotterdam and its 300 years of history would have been leveled.

As the tugs nudge the huge ship sideways up to the dock, the crewmen heave small lines, which tied to the huge hawsers and snaked to the dock then mechanically tightened to precisely the right tension, allowing for the rise and fall of the North Sea tide. The spring lines follow, and in a matter of minutes the ship is docked, and the crew can stop work and look out over the busy harbor. A triple blast of the ship's horn announces the end of the docking maneuver and the beginning of shore leave for those whose watch schedule permits it.

Captain Zhakdin too will take a brief turn ashore, before the loading and unloading begin. He has an hour and a half to find a shop and locate an electronic game his daughter has requested. It is Sunday, and he hopes the computer store is open. He walks briskly along the streets, stopping to ask directions in his accented English and surprised that every person he stops speaks the international language with such ease. When he finally finds the shop, he is glad it is open, unaware that more and more Dutch shop owners are keeping their shops open on Sunday, despite resistance from religious groups with dwindling power over commerce in this thoroughly modern country with a history of heavy-handed religious influence.

Zhakdin has little difficulty talking to the clerk, and the requested toy is produced. Only the price is a surprise. The device sells for more than he expected, and he must use a credit card, which he sees as an unnecessarily Western method of payment, introducing a risk of overspending. But he has spent considerable time and effort to find the game, and he always enjoys buying things for his daughter because of the way her face lights up when she opens his gifts. So he uses the credit card and is pleased. He can afford to spend the money. He will not be back in St. Petersburg for two weeks, but his wife can pay the bills as she usually does when he is away.

Carrying the newly purchased game under his arm, he hurries back to his ship to supervise the unloading of the containers destined for Europe and the loading of more for America. When he arrives at the dock, the truck ramp has been brought into place, and the trucks are already waiting in line, the drivers outside chatting over coffee and enjoying the rare sunshine that warms and dries this frequently rainy city. Some of the truckers have gone into a tavern, strategically located next to the truck queue. Captain Zhakdin pays little attention to them as he hurries to the ship. The crew is not to begin unloading until he returns.

The crane operator is in the cab, and the ramp is in place, so only his go-ahead is required, and he gives it as soon as he can see safety precautions have been taken — the balance weights of the crane, the men wearing hard hats, the spotters in position. At his signal the crane operator swings his hook over the stacked containers and unlocks the corners, and crewmen swarm around the stack, placing the belts so the containers can be hoisted. The officer directing the operation works from a sheaf of bills of lading, one for each container, and a computer terminal that shows a three-dimensional view of the ship's load. He can locate any of the containers in an instant. The containers loaded in St. Petersburg were carefully placed so that those slated to come off in Rotterdam are on top.

The trucks roll up the ramp and into position next to the crane. The containers are hoisted up, pulled along an overhead rail across the top of the stack until they're above the line of trucks, moved forward or aft to where the next truck is then lowered, maneuvered into position by crewmen, and ratcheted down to the flatbed before the trucks drive off. Occasionally a truck is out of sequence, but this is no problem. The crane simply deposits the container on the errant truck, which then has to wait until the trucks ahead of it are loaded. The operation goes rapidly because of the careful loading in St. Petersburg and the computer listing of each container's position. About a third of the containers are offloaded for distribution to various cities in Holland, Belgium, and Germany. The top two layers of containers are removed, leaving the mustard-yellow container exposed for the first time since they covered it in St. Petersburg.

A blast of the ship's horn signals the offloading has been completed and the loading of containers destined for the U.S.

can begin. The loaded trucks are already lined up in another queue, and as soon as the last offloading truck has cleared the ramp, the loading trucks roll on to deposit their containers. The crane then reverses its operation, plucking the containers off the waiting trucks and depositing them in the fourth and fifth tiers of the stack. As each container is deposited and locked down, a record of its position is entered into a computer file that keeps information about the hold and its cargo.

At the beginning of the loading operation, several crewmembers walk across the mustard-yellow container, and at the right moment, they signal to the crane operator, who locks a container of the fourth layer directly to it.

The entire offloading and loading operations are performed in a day, and the ship is ready to sail by Sunday evening. Captain Zhakdin, however, decides to wait until morning so they can leave in the daylight, which is safer for harbor navigation, and gives the crew an opportunity to spend a night ashore. This will result, he knows, in a certain amount of drunkenness among the crew and resultant hangovers diminishing performance the next day, but he feels the loss is outweighed by the additional safety of clearing the harbor in daylight.

9. THE OTHER STORY HITS

Sunday. Greenwich Village, New York,

I'm having breakfast in a small coffee shop on 10th St., just around the corner from my old apartment. It's where I go for breakfast when I don't feel like making it myself, which is often. Convenience was its main asset back when I lived in the Village. Now it's a trek, but some habits aren't easily broken. Besides the great coffee, they know me. I like that.

I've brought a *Sunday Post* from the newsstand on the corner. The *Washington Post* is our competition in a way. Not for sales of course; they're in Washington. But we do compete for prestige. The *Post* is a good paper, well written and with excellent editors who know how to put a paper together. In national politics they outshine the *Times* because they're right there where it's all happening, though these days, I think it's more "not working" than anything. On page three a headline catches my eye, and I fold the paper vertically down the middle so I can read it without dipping it in my eggs.

Pentagon Official Finds Fraud
By David McWhalen

Washington, D.C., September 1 —There is something rotten in the Pentagon, recently uncovered by an army colonel. Col. R. R. Haldane sits in an important chair at the Pentagon. She checks to see if contracts have been awarded fairly and legally. If all is well, she approves them. By law the decision to enter into a contract for purchase from a supplier can only occur after three bids. The contract must go to the lowest bidder, unless a compelling argument can be made that the higher price brings some additional value. In other words Col. Haldane makes sure your tax dollars are spent wisely and within the law.

In the past few months, however, Col. Haldane found three contracts wanting. In one case, there had been no bidding at all. This lack could have been justified by expediency, particularly in a time of war. However the country is not in a state of war, as legally determined. More importantly from the legal point of view, no rationale for bypassing the bidding was presented.

In another case, the contract had been given to the highest bidder without a rationale for paying the higher price. In the third case, the contract was awarded for a clearly inferior product, and the price was higher as well. Col. Haldane sent all three contracts back to the appropriate office and requested that the procedures required by law be followed before she would approve them.

One other fact raised additional questions. Each of these three contracts was given to a company previously controlled by the current vice president, Richard Bentley. So, Col. Haldane reasoned, there was the appearance of fraud, and to protect the vice president from this appearance, it was particularly important that the bidding process be followed.

Soon after she returned the contracts for revision, they were back on her desk again, still missing the requisite arguments. Attached to the contracts was a brief note telling her to move forward. She called the head of the legal department, with the intention of beginning an internal investigation, which was the next step required by the department's regulations, but he refused to speak with her.

"I had no choice but to disapprove the contracts," she said to this reporter. "If I were to approve them, I would become a part of an illegal activity, and neither my conscience nor my father's voice — and they may be the same thing — would allow that." As she made this remark, there was a smile on the face of this tall and impressive officer, born into a poor New York family and trained in the law.

By speaking to this reporter, however, Col. Haldane has moved forward in another way.

My eggs arrived halfway through the story. They were a bit runny, but I was hungry. The bagel, however, was wonderful. You can't get bagels this good anywhere but New York City, and there are places where you can't get bagels at all, I've been told. Next to the bagel sits a little square blob of cream cheese. Some people think you have to put cream cheese on a bagel, but you don't. Butter is better.

I order another bagel and more coffee. Munching and slurping I think about this army colonel who has just crossed swords with one of the most powerful men in Washington. She's going to get in trouble — big trouble. I wonder how big. She can be removed permanently from her position. Probably, however, Vice President Bentley will want everyone to know he was responsible for her removal. He wants to be feared more than anything else. I read Machiavelli when I was in college, and I'm pretty sure VP Bentley follows his advice.

Interrupting my Machiavellian reminiscing, I see a text from Max Josephthal, my lawyer buddy. "Call me," it says.

***

I call his office. Max himself answers. Of course he does; it's Sunday. And he lives where he works.

"Come right over," he tells me. "How soon can you get here? Grab today's *Post* on your way."

"I'm on 10ᵗʰ St. I'll get a cab." I tuck my paper in my bag.

When I get to his office, there's no typical repartee. Max has his serious demeanor on.

He sits back down in his rocking, swiveling, rolling, everything-but-give-you-a-massage office chair and puts his hands behind his head and looks at me, right in the eyes. "You see this morning's *Post*?" And I see him tap his finger on the headline of the Col. Haldane story I'd just read.

"I did."

"She's my client. I want you to meet her. Write about her. Call her. She can fill you in on what you might be missing for your container-ship story."

"What's her story?" I ask as Max hands me her business card. "There's always more info than makes it into the first story."

"She's been getting screwed over by the powers that be. And we all know who that is. She was here just an hour ago. I thought I'd introduce you, but she left before you came. Maybe you passed her in the lobby."

I shake my head. "That's too bad. I'd like to meet her."

"I've known Roxie all her life; grew up with her father. She came to me when she knew she'd be going public with this story; just wanted to be smart about it. This *Post* story is just the beginning. Now we see how the boys will play it."

"Can you make her case?"

He chuckles. "We expected retribution and we won't have any trouble proving it. So if she gets canned, she'll get her job back. But it won't work that way. She won't lose her job; she'll get demoted, something to embarrass her, shut her up."

"And they can get away with that? Why?"

"Because they really are corrupt, power-hungry bastards, to

put a fine point on it." He smiles at his little witticism.

"Sure." I smile back. "We know that. Even the public seems to know that. That story is an old story. Corruption's become so commonplace, people don't seem to think twice about it."

"You think the people don't care their leaders are corrupt?" His voice rises a little, and I can see it's a topic that makes him angry.

"I don't know. They care, but not as much. And there's another thing." I hesitate, not sure if I want to take the time to go into my analysis of the world.

"What's that?" He invites, and I plunge in.

"People are way more political than they used to be, more committed to party politics, more convinced the other side is evil. As a result they keep supporting them, even when they're obviously corrupt. It's a bad trend. Bad for the country." I conclude my little speech.

"Yeah, you're right about that. Even if I prove Vice President Bentley's old cronies are as crooked as French pimps, the faithful will keep supporting him. And he knows that, so he can go on pushing his weight around. It'll be next to impossible to pick a jury that can agree, so we'll probably settle. It's usually better anyway. But the opposition won't settle very fairly. They think they have all the power on their side."

"Don't they?"

"Not all of it. But they have a lot of it."

"What have you got on the VP?"

"Off the record? Sorry I have to ask."

"Sure."

"I have copies of emails the vice president sent to the commanding general, telling him to get 'that black bitch,' as he put it, out of procurement."

"That should help. Sounds like they were on to her before

the story broke."

"We know so. It should help, but it won't. All they need is one of these rabid conservatives on the jury to toe the party line, and the jury will hang." He hesitates. "And if they don't get a stubborn jury member, they can hire one. Money buys a lot of stubbornness."

"What can they argue?"

"They can say that bypassing the usual bidding procedures was required to streamline the war on terrorism. That sells a lot of chicken parts."

I could feel my mouth starting to form the question "Chicken parts?" But he goes on.

"The woman comes off looking as though she's soft on terrorism, and in today's climate a lot of people will believe it and agree she should be demoted or fired. Saying someone is soft on terrorism these days is just like saying they were soft on communism in the McCarthy era. Nobody questions the motives of the guy making the accusation. They're too scared. The guys on the right know this, and they're using it wherever they can."

It's a long speech for Max, but I watch his brown eyes flame up toward the end. It's something he's passionate about.

"Well, good luck on it. And thanks for the info. I'll give her a call." I get up and tug my jeans down a bit, seeing his eyes follow my hands and think it's great that he's such a good guy *and* he has a working libido. Not my type, though I do like older men. And I've got one already.

10. THE VICE PRESIDENT'S OFFICE

Sunday, Late Morning. Washington, D.C.

"She's not a team player, is she?" The aide taps his finger hard on the open newspaper lying flat on his boss' desk. The VP reads the headline, "Pentagon Official Finds Fraud," wearing his famous scowl.

"No, she's not." His voice is low and steady as he skims the story. The aide hears a threat. The VP keeps his cool. That shows his superiority.

"Fire her," the VP says.

"Won't that raise a few eyebrows?"

"Of course it'll raise eyebrows. I didn't get this job because I'm afraid of raising eyebrows." The aide notes he is starting to lose the carefully cultured cool.

"I don't give a rat's ass about eyebrows."

"Well, actually," the aide says, "it's more than that. There's the whistleblower law. She could bring charges."

"I don't give a fuck if she brings charges. They won't stick. We can buy any judge, any jury, any congressional committee. We can buy the whole damned country's opinion, if we need to, with an advertising campaign. We did that in the election. Remember?"

He glances at the aide as if he considered him a cretin to have forgotten the great victory of the election, when they had hoodwinked the public with television ads.

"We don't have to worry about things like whistleblower laws. They don't apply to us now. We're at war."

"All right, I'll call Benny today," referring to the secretary of defense.

"Do that. Give the bitch a week to get her stuff out of the office. I want her dishonorably discharged. Ask Benny if he thinks he could make a bigger charge stick — dereliction of duty, maybe, or treason. Not just failure to obey. That's wussy stuff. She's done worse than that. I want her record tainted, so she'll find it hard to get a job."

"Yes, sir." The aide smiles a little. His boss is tough, one of the meanest, toughest guys in politics, and the aide admires him. Vice President Bentley would never again run for office; he was too old. This position will be his last, so he can do whatever he likes without worrying about public opinion. And as for legality, as he said, they can buy anyone who stands in the way.

The aide walks thoughtfully back through the corridor to his office, smiling to himself. He loves being close to power. It is a thrill like no other; better, he thinks, than actually having the power, because the person with the power has to be careful about the law, politics, public opinion, and many other things. Of course his boss is different about this. Still, he's glad not to be sitting at his boss' desk; he prefers being close to the energy, warming his bony behind at the fireside.

But when he gets to his office, he sees the VP has sent him a memo.

"OK. You win," he grumbles. "Just have her demoted. But she still has to move to another office, down where the little people work."

11. NEW YORK CITY

Monday

My office is a mess, as always, but I like sitting at the desk surveying my little kingdom. A good computer and a landline and I can get the background on just about any story. I bring up my email. It's the usual crap. I subscribe electronically to half a dozen other papers, just to make sure I haven't missed anything or slanted something the wrong way. It takes an hour and a half to skim through all of them. The *Washington Post* seems to be the only one covering the story about Col. Haldane, and they haven't given it much priority. It's just another story about the government running amok with arrogance. It doesn't matter that there's a law protecting whistleblowers against retaliation; the guys in charge know no one's going to care if they break it. Well, I care, I think to myself, and I'll write an article that will shrivel their testicles into dried currants.

First, I research Col. Haldane. I've got her phone number and email, thanks to Max, but I want to see what the world says about her first.

All the information on her is marked "R.R. Haldane," as if she has no first name, and I wonder if she's trying to hide one of those embarrassing monikers parents give their children sometimes. I try a few out — "Ronkonkama Romp Haldane" after a wild weekend. Or "Really Resourceful Haldane" because they wanted her to be ready for anything. Or just "Rosalie Regina" because they were technogeeks and totally out of touch with contemporary culture. I give up in the end and read on.

She was born and brought up right here in NYC, in Queens.

Her father was a bus driver, and her mom got into law school, which wasn't bad for a woman in the '50s, but dropped out because she couldn't pay for more than the first semester. Too bad. She would have been a pioneer. R.R. had no brothers or sisters. She was a crackerjack student in the public schools and an athlete besides. She played women's basketball when it was just starting to be popular and could have gone on to help forge the new professional league, but she was too smart to give up on her education. She went on to college at a CUNY branch. It was a low-cost option for the Haldanes but definitely a place to get a decent education. While there, she discovered the ROTC program, which had almost died during the '60s anti-Vietnam War protest era 30 years earlier.

ROTC was still weak, and few students sought it out, but R.R. seemed to enjoy going in a different direction. She also discovered that by joining the army, she could get a lot of practical experience in leadership and free courses on almost any subject she wanted to know about. Her mother's dream of law school swam before her eyes, and after she graduated from CUNY, the army paid for her to go to Columbia Law, in exchange for which she promised to give some years to the service. She finished in the top five of her class and passed the bar on the first try. She decided to fulfill her obligation to the army before clerking for a judge, but she was surprised to discover she liked the discipline and structure of the army. She was suddenly happy, and it was a new feeling. As a tall, strong girl in high school who was smarter than all of her classmates, she hadn't found it easy to fit in. In the army she not only fit in, but she was appreciated, and she knew right where she belonged at any given moment. It was a great match of talent, personality, need, and obligation.

Her career in the army was one of promotion after promotion, in which she excelled at each level. When she made colonel, the promotion came with an offer — a post in procurement in the Pentagon. She was glad for the opportunity to apply her legal expertise and her leadership skills, and she rose in the agency. She'd been in the job for three years when she ran afoul of the vice president's men trying to make mountains of dollars out of reconstruction in the Middle East, and she found it impossible to reconcile the debt she felt she owed her country with the shenanigans going on around her, based on greed.

I'm consumed by this topic, as I generally am when I get a good story, and suddenly it's three in the afternoon, long past lunchtime, but I'm not hungry. I'm angry. I take a wee break and eat a candy bar. Not good. Not good. But good. I have my little internal debate about food all the time, and I wonder who it is that wins them. Or loses them. I lick the last little remnants of chocolate off my fingertips, wipe them on my jeans, and call Tom.

***

"What's up?" he asks when he picks up his phone. I'm glad he has my number in his contacts.

"I'm working on this whistleblower lady in the Pentagon."

"Yeah, I read about it."

"You got anything helpful?"

"Have you talked to her yet?"

"Not yet, but soon. It looks as though Bentley's boys are running the procurement business down there. And raking it in."

"Procurement, huh? You know, in law enforcement, that word spells pimp."

"And the lady decided not to put out."

"On the street she'd be in big trouble."

"Well, she is."

"I'll see what I can find out."

"Thanks." I wait until the grin has faded from my face, and I call the lady colonel.

***

"Colonel Haldane's office." A deep, velvety, male voice answers.

I'm using my hands-free set so I'm ready to key in at the drop of a hat, but when I hear that voice, my hands check my neckline buttons. I wonder if the colonel likes his voice as much as I do. She probably doesn't have time for more than a passing tingle, I think.

"This is Kimberly Hansen at the *New York Times*." I try to sound feminine then check myself, remembering Tom. "Does she have any time?"

"I think the colonel will want to make time for the *Times*." In the two vowels in "time," I hear an echo of the South that warms my morning bagel. I can feel the butter melting.

"Thank you, uh, what's your name?" And I think, You're bad, Kimmie, you're really bad.

"I'm Edward, ma'am, Chief Petty Officer Edward Timmons," the velvet bass replies. He knows what I'm thinking. With a voice like that, it must happen every day.

"Thanks for your help, Edward."

"No problem, ma'am. I'll put you through to Colonel Haldane."

"Thanks." There's a brief silence.

"This is Colonel Haldane." Very businesslike but a little tired, I think.

"Good morning, Colonel. I'm Kimmie Hansen, of the *Times*."

"So Edward said."

"Mmm, hmmm, good," I answer, meaning it's good he told her, but it comes out as if I'm smacking my lips over Edward.

"Max said you'd call. Where shall we start?" I can hear the smile in her voice at my unintended meaning.

"First, how are you holding up?" I've done some other whistleblower stories, and it's a wearing-down business. The hostility is all around, and it nibbles away at a person's energy. Not many can put up with it. Hearing the colonel's voice, however, I think she might be able to.

"It's harder than I thought it would be. I'm a tough old bird. I've seen shit you haven't dreamed of, but it's hard feeling all this hatred being beamed at me like a field-weapon laser."

"That's what I've heard from others in the same boat. Are those lasers coming from any particular directions?"

"From several different directions. Off the record, Vice President Bentley has placed some of his men throughout the Procurement Department. They're like spies."

"That tells me your department is uppermost in his mind."

"No question about it. He's over here himself a lot too. If you want a good story, see if you can figure out how he's going to profit from all these contracts. I know he's divested himself from the company. He had to during the election. But he must be making big personal money from these contracts. There's no other way to explain the intensity of his interest in this department."

"Thanks for the tip. It's a line of investigation any reporter would pursue."

"Yes, sure, I know that, but somehow there's more to it in this case than usual."

I understand what she's saying, and I think I should do some investigation, get more of the details under my belt, then talk to her again.

"You've got yourself some powerful enemies. I'll take your advice and follow the money trail. I assume you don't want to be quoted on this."

"You got that right. They'd send me so far down, I wouldn't be able to hear the flush."

"No problem. It'll be 'anonymous sources in the Pentagon.'"

"Good. I'll call you if I have anything for you. I always read the *Times*."

"Thanks, Colonel. Say goodbye to Edward for me."

She chuckles. "I'll do that."

We're on our way to being buds. I give her my email address.

The facts had already come out in the *Post*'s story: She'd given a big contract to "another" company, not the VP's. She was following procedure, giving the job to the company with the lowest bid, trying to save the American people's nickel. But that wasn't what the VP's people wanted her to do. They wanted her to "expedite," which meant giving the contract to his old company even though it had submitted a higher bid. As a result, she got demoted for "incompetence." Now she no longer makes the decisions about who gets a contract. Instead, she's assembling bids, just a mechanical job really, and writing a report on them to a guy — one of the VP's men — who now sits in what used to be her chair.

The *Post* broke the story first; I'm planning a follow-up, digging a little deeper, filling in a few more of the details. I punch up a list of recent appointments and changes in the Pentagon and try to figure out who the VP's men are.

The only one I can be sure of is the guy who's now holding the job she used to have. I call him, but he isn't in. Instead, I have a little chat with his secretary, Annette, a civilian, about how much she likes her new job. I have the impression she's never done real secretarial work before and can probably count to maybe ten without too much outside help. She can't stop talking about how much she admires her new boss, John Embry, also a civilian, who's trying to streamline the procurement of contracts for the army so our boys over there will be able to defend themselves. I can see he doesn't trust her, because he's given her the same line he gives the public. We have a nice chat, but she doesn't know anything worth putting in the story.

But I can tell her new boss is up to no good.

12. KIMMIE AND ROXIE

Monday, Lunchtime. Washington, D.C.

I come in from the rain, shuck my coat and hat. My hair is still wet on the sides, and I walk to my desk, turning my head first to one side then the other while I dry the sides by fluffing them with splayed fingers. The mess on my desk is familiar, and I'm glad to see it. It's my real home.

I touch the space bar, and my computer wakes up, bright and perky, ready to work. I love computers; they don't need coffee and small talk in the morning, and they don't expect flowers or lunch on Secretaries' Day. There's email — one from my little sister in San Francisco, pregnant again. That woman. This'll be her fifth. I hoped the last one would be her last. I love my nephews and nieces, but five is too many for anyone. Her husband is helpful, however, and that makes a difference. Still. Five. Too many. I send her a message saying scientists have now figured out what causes pregnancy, and she should consider watching TV in the evenings. She's probably tried that. The problem is, her husband's such a nice guy.

There's a note from Col. Haldane suggesting lunch together somewhere in the District. Bingo, I think. That sounds juicy. Otherwise, why would she want to meet me away from her office?

I call right away, and Edward answers. I flirt with him a little, just to stay in practice, before explaining that the colonel asked me to call.

"She's expecting your call." He makes those five words sound dark and sweet, like the smell of piney woods at sunset. I could take a little nap in those woods. "Don't go there," I say to myself. Then, out loud, "Thank you, Edward," failing to match him for sexiness.

"Colonel. Haldane." I hear her clipped, businesslike voice.

"It's Kimmie Hansen."

"Yes, good. Glad you called back. Are we on for lunch?"

"I can be in D.C. by 1:00 today."

"That would be perfect. There's a little lunch place on M and 17th called Luciano's. It'll be quiet." I know she means her colleagues won't be there. "Is that OK?"

"It sounds fine."

"OK then. I'll see you there around 1:00."

I call Amtrak and make a reservation for the ten o'clock train. I can just make it. I glance quickly at the rest of my email, figure it'll have to wait, and turn off my terminal.

On my way out, I pop my head in Jim's office.

"I'm off to Washington. Back tonight."

"Right." He waves his hand then looks up. "Whistleblower?"

"Yup."

"Good luck."

Jim Langdon, my editor, is a super-talented journalist and works very hard, a great boss to have, but I'm glad I'm not married to him. The *Times* is his life.

The rain hasn't let up, and I walk quickly to the corner, where it's easier to get a cab. It takes a while anyway. In the rain cabs are suddenly filled with people who don't want to wait for a bus. Eventually one stops, and I get in.

"Grand Central," I say, and he rockets off. I decide not to shake my head and sprinkle water all over the cab's interior. He drives fast, and I try not to think about the slick streets. The ride seems short, considering the rain, and he lets me out right at the entrance to Grand Central so I don't have to get any wetter. I increase my usual tip.

In the huge hall, the ceiling 60-70 feet high, the echoes of high heels on marble ricochet around the room at the speed of sound. The information sign dominates the landscape. My train is delayed only ten minutes, not bad for New York in the rain. Amtrak is trying. I wonder, however, why rain should make a train late. I just can't see it. Are those big steel wheels intimidated by the little drops of water on the rails?

Waiting for the train's announcement, I start piecing together parts of the story, based on the few words the colonel and I had before, about how she felt those laser-like looks all the time. I like the sound of "laser-like looks," and I'm thinking how to put them in the story when the announcement booms and I go down the stairs to the tracks. The waiting train looks big and powerful. No prissy raindrops will keep it from getting to Washington. I'm one of the first on and get a good seat, meaning it faces forward and the seat next to it's empty, so I can use it like a little desk, piling up papers with ideas, lines, quotations. I do this to discourage people from sitting next to me. They'd have to ask me to move my stuff, and it's easier just to find another seat.

The train stops only once, somewhere in New Jersey. I quickly tire of trying to write the story without the information and go off into daydreams. Tom's personality, Gaylord's body, and Edward's voice are all combined somehow as I fall asleep with my head against the window. I wake up every time the train goes over a little bump. Then I fall asleep deeply and wake up with a start as we pull into Union Station. I stumble out of the car, up and out of the station, and hail a cab. The cabbie grunts when I tell him the address, and I feel right at home.

Luciano's is an unobtrusive little help-yourself luncheonette in an out-of-the-way part of the district. I get there by 12:45

and grab a cup of coffee from one of those pumper pots to get my brain working. Col. Haldane comes in right at 1:00. She's almost six feet tall and broad shouldered. Very imposing, in fact. I smile and hold out my hand just as she takes off her overcoat and hangs it up, which takes both of her hands out of shaking range.

Everyone in the luncheonette stares at the uniform first. Even if you don't know what all of it means, you can tell she's special because she has extra stripes and little brass things on her uniform. Then people look at her face. She's a light brown African-American woman with a look that would be called handsome. A big, open face. Eyes wide apart. A large mouth which smiles as we finally shake hands. She oozes competence and authority mixed with easygoing friendliness. I want her to be president. Yeah right; it'll be a while before a black woman gets to be president. Still, it could happen. She has my vote.

We move to the order line, and I have to squint to see the menu. I also have to be careful ordering because I sit for a living, and the part of me that sits is growing faster than the other parts. So I start to order a little green salad, but then my appetite gets the better of me, and I order a big salad with meat and cheese in it. She orders a burger and fries. We're probably matched for calories, but I'm sure she works out every day in a big gym in the Pentagon, while I get my exercise running for buses and raising my arm to hail taxis.

We go wait in another line to get our food and make some chatter about the weather. It's no better here than in New York. Once we've sat down, she's all business. I notice she looks carefully around the restaurant at each one of the patrons, sizing them up.

Between mouthfuls I first get a quick update on her situation — no change. Then I say, "So, you know my friend Max?"

"My father grew up with Max. Best friends actually."

"In Queens, yes?" I add, a bit embarrassed I already learned this off the Internet.

"I always loved the stories he'd tell me of the two of them roaming the streets of New York."

"They must have been an unlikely pair of friends, I guess, a Lower-East-Side Jew and a Harlem black. There certainly weren't many friendships like that in those days. Maybe it's different now."

"It's a little different, but it would still be an unusual friendship. They thought they could change the world — end racism and anti-Semitism just by being who they were."

"I'm sure they made a contribution."

"Well, I don't know. Their ambitions were bigger than they were, I'm afraid. But then, that's the thing about ambitions, I think. We grow into them."

Then she changes her tone.

"OK. Here's what I want to talk to you about." We both lean forward. "We're trying to develop a method for intercepting explosives and other things, but mostly explosives, from container ships."

"I know. Max told me. In fact, I'm developing a story on it. Or trying to."

"So you know the main problem."

"Inspection?"

"Well, yes, in a way. But it's really a bigger problem than that. Containers are packed wherever their contents are produced, then driven by truck to the dock. If they're going on a large container ship, they're hoisted up by a dockside crane and stacked on the ship. But the smaller ships use a roll-on / roll-off method."

"RoRo," I say, proud I know the basics.

"Obviously, they're the ones we're worried about. A bomb could be headed for a major city in less than a minute. It's so fast there's no time to inspect the cargo."

"How about afterwards. In the yard?"

"That'd create a huge bottleneck."

I nod.

"Up to now we've only been doing spot checks, and not enough of those."

"Could they be inspected while the ship is at sea?"

"Yes, but it's difficult and time-consuming. Most of the containers are buried under other containers."

"Could—"

She interrupts and keeps me from making another creative suggestion. "We're developing systems to inspect the cargo on the ground, where the container is packed."

"But how do you control that? They're being packed all over the place."

"There are four parts to the system," she says, and I know I'm going to learn everything I need to know about it. "First, international agreements with all the exporting countries. Second, a smart tag goes on every item in the container; the tag has weight, dimensions, general descriptions, place of origin and destination, and the name and location of the person who inspected it. Third, a new device, combining laser and ultrasound technology scans the contents of the container, analyzes it, and sends the data to the fourth element, a computer program on the ship searches for discrepancies, even does a spectral and radioactivity analysis of individual items. If something doesn't match the list of loaded items, we'll know. All this takes place at sea. If something's wrong, we order the ship to stand off and wait for clearance. If the problem isn't resolved, we send it back."

"That sounds great, but what if the guy loading the container gets bribed to mislabel something, or look the other way?"

"One of the beauties of the system is we deputize a specific employee of the company as a temporary U.S. Customs officer. That means he gives his name and address to the U.S. government, and we can check on him. He gets a small payment from us on top of his salary from the company. Of course, people can lie, set up false identities, etc., but we can uncover these if we have the manpower to check up on them. With the list of TCOs, we have the authority to manage the loading of every container that's destined for the U.S. It costs very little, and the computer can search the records. If anything looks a little funny, we can fire the guy and ask the company for a replacement. If we catch them misrepresenting the cargo, or letting something into the container that shouldn't be there, they're subject to U.S. law. This is a powerful deterrent to the small-time smuggler and the bribe taker, but of course it doesn't mean squat to the real terrorist."

"So, how do you protect us from the real terrorist?"

"Well, first, if we find a fake identity, we just kick him off the list, alert the local authorities, and let them handle it, or not. But the main weapon against the real terrorist is the shipboard device that analyzes each container and compares its bill of lading with the cargo for dimensions, radioactivity, and density."

"Why is density important?"

"The spectral and density analyses will uncover both regular explosives and nuclear devices."

"How can you be so sure?"

"There's only one type of nuclear device a terrorist could possibly put together —- what's called a 'gun-barrel' type." She pauses for a second and looks at me. "How much do you know about nuclear devices?"

I choke back a wise-ass reply. Instead, I say, "Not anywhere near enough, I'm sure, but I can find out."

"Well, the military ones are way beyond the reach of terrorists — too expensive, too complex, too big to transport. The only type they could make is what the nuclear guys used to call Little Boys, where a conventional explosion sends a chunk of uranium-235 down a 'gun barrel' so it crashes at high speed into another chunk of uranium-235, causing a chain reaction. And because it's confined inside the walls of this bomb, the chain reaction makes a massive explosion. Nothing compared to a hydrogen bomb, but still plenty big enough and potentially very damaging to a metropolitan area. It's the kind that devastated Hiroshima."

"OK, so it has to be a Little Boy."

"Right. And the key to identifying one is in the radioactivity and the density of the material. If we can make an analysis, we can spot it."

"And the on-board device makes this analysis?"

"Exactly. There's a small piece of hardware inside each container that performs the analysis and sends the results to an on-board computer. Once the cargo is loaded on the ship, the security officer runs the program and gets a report on the contents of every container."

"Why wait until it's on the ship?"

"First, to allow the ship to be loaded quickly. Efficiency is everything in the cargo business. But more importantly, because once the ship is at sea, we have complete control over its location. We can order it to stand offshore and stay there. We can bring another container ship — an empty one — alongside, transfer all the clean containers by crane until we get down to the suspicious one and inspect it visually. Then we can scuttle it — just drop it in the water and let it sink. Even if it goes off, it'll do only minimal damage."

I make a mental note that the military's idea of minimal damage might be different from a Greenpeace member's.

"OK. I understand the system. What did you want to write up?"

"We sent out bids on the devices that get installed in the containers. They aren't very complicated, but you can imagine the quantity — there's one in every container. So there's big money to be made from supplying Homeland Security with them."

"I can guess the rest. When you sent out the request for bids, Bentley's company bid higher than the competition, but his guys in the Pentagon wanted you to give them the contract anyway."

"You've got half of it. The other half is that the equipment the VP's company makes doesn't do as good a job. Their equipment can compare the dimensions, can locate the item, identify the packer, all of that. But it can't do the full analysis. It can't do the density / radioactivity analysis. It costs money to include that analysis component. By leaving it out, they make more profit."

"But — did I get this right? — that's the component that identifies the nuclear device?"

"That's right. To put it bluntly, the VP's company is making more money by leaving the U.S. vulnerable to a nuclear attack."

"Didn't you say they bid higher than the competition?"

"Yes, I did. They're greedy. They bid high then force the contract through, claiming it's an emergency, but they leave out the one component that does the most important job, just to make a few extra bucks."

"This is a big story."

"It is. It shouldn't have happened, but it did. It's exactly what got me demoted. I called them on it publicly, and they demoted me. Of course that's illegal, but they don't care. Their device has already been approved. I don't know who approved it, or why. I can't even find out when it was approved. They think they have all the power. Even if there's a congressional investigation, they have the votes to defeat, or at least postpone, it. They just don't care whether it's legal or not."

As she talks, she gets more and more animated. She keeps her cool in that military way they all seem to have, but I can tell she's filled with indignant fury. It shines right out of her eyes. To me, she's a real patriot, trying to save her country from terrorists. The VP's men are greedy vultures, feeding off the anxiety the country feels, and they're protected by a coalition of conservative senators and congressmen. I not only pick up on her anger, I also start to feel it myself.

I'm going to enjoy writing the story.

All the time she's been talking, she's been taking bites of her burger and fries, and when she's done telling her story, her plate's clean. I, on the other hand, sit there with my mouth hanging open, taking notes, and ignoring my lunch.

"I have to get back," Haldane says. "They notice if I'm gone too long. Give me a ring if you need anything explained, but don't send email. They read that. And I'll probably have to switch to a different phone line, but that's easy enough."

"Thanks. Thanks a lot. It's a privilege to write about it." I'm gushing a little, but I don't care. She's a heroic figure, and I'm in awe.

She stands up, getting ready to leave.

I stand up to shake her hand.

She smiles, and I know she's pleased I understand what she's doing, but there's something in her smile, a little sadness, that tells me she doesn't think her career in the army will survive this second story. She gets her coat and leaves, giving me a little wave at the door.

After she leaves, I eat my salad, but it doesn't taste that good.

13. ON THE TRAIN HOME

Monday

I ride back to New York excited by this story. There's a guy next to me, so I can't spread out. There's just the little tray table, and my lap. But that's not a problem. I don't need to write anything down. My head is full of ideas. I'm so excited by this story, it feels as though my head is floating around toward the domed ceiling of the train car.

The train bounces and sways. The smell of some passenger's home-made meal spreads through the coach, but it distracts me only for a second. I sit back and put phrases together in my mind as I stare out the window at the blurred scenery. I recall the notes I took during lunch, firming up the problem in my head. It really isn't complicated and shouldn't be hard to write. I think of some questions I want to ask the colonel when I get another chance. Outside the streaky window, ugly parts of Maryland, Delaware, and then New Jersey fly by, but I might as well be in Nepal.

I imagine a bomb going off in Manhattan. Maybe the buildings would contain some of the blast. Modern buildings would be stronger than Hiroshima's in the '40s. But it would still destroy whole buildings and all the people in them. Afterwards the radiation would drift on dainty breezes into windows, through playgrounds, over the rivers, into New Jersey or Connecticut or Westchester, silently killing as it drifted.

I sit still and quiet, thinking about the code name Little Boy. I know how cruel little boys can be, and how innocent they can appear. The train pulls into a station, and my seatmate gets off. My head comes back down to reality, and I open my laptop and log on, reading about nuclear bombs, how they're made, and how they were used at the end of World War II. In a few hours, I'll be back in New York, sitting at my office computer, and then I'll start writing. The phrases will pop out of my fingertips as needed. It's a process I enjoy. Much of my stories get drafted in my head before I ever put a word on paper. But just to get the facts organized, I write out a story about the Hiroshima bomb. Maybe I'll even get it published. Probably not. It's been told a thousand times.

Dropping the Bomb in '45
By Kimberly Hansen

It has been many years since Hiroshima and Nagasaki, and many Americans may have forgotten the story. But it's not a story we should ever forget.

It began very early on the morning of August 6, 1945 on the island of Tinian in the Pacific. Col. Tibbets and his handpicked crew had been training in the States while their plane was being outfitted to carry its extraordinary cargo. It was clearly the most important mission of the war. He and his crew were going to drop the first atomic bomb on the city of Hiroshima, and he had chosen to pilot the plane himself. If it exploded with the expected force, and rumor said it was the biggest bomb ever made, it could cow the Japanese into surrendering, before U.S. troops invaded on the ground. How could he not be the pilot for that mission?

The president — Harry S. Truman — had approved the mission; undoubtedly the most important, and the most difficult, decision of his presidency. He knew the consequences if the mission were successful — many civilian Japanese dead — and he balanced that consequence against the alternative — many American soldiers killed during an invasion of Japan. In those days the Japanese were seen as monsters. They had raped China, performed inhumane atrocities on their prisoners, and attacked America without warning. These images may have helped the president conclude the bomb should be dropped. His regrets would come later.

At the airport on Tinian, the bomb had already been loaded. The colonel had named the plane after his mother, Enola Gay, but why? Did he think of her as carrying some lethal force? Was his plane the "mother ship?" Probably he just missed her.

One bomb. That's all they were going to drop. They boarded at 2:00 a.m., breathlessly excited, brave, sure of their skill. The B-29 Superfortress was a good ship, one of the best bombers the U.S. had produced, and it had several new features. The pilot could control the gunnery from the cockpit, a task left in earlier planes to the bombardier, and the engines were bigger and more reliable. The load this time was heavy, but not heavier than the usual complement of smaller bombs. But this was one colossal bomb. Its size demanded special remodeling of the bomb bay doors and release mechanism.

They took off, climbed to cruising altitude, and found their easterly heading. The flight across the western Pacific was uneventful. They gave their position periodically to the controller at the base, but it was all routine, and boring. But after many hours of straight flight, the city of Hiroshima appeared in front of them, and they knew what they had to do. Their adrenalin surged.

They didn't know the residents of the city had already received two alarms that bombers were flying over the city.

Both warnings had come to nothing, so most people ignored the approach of the *Enola Gay* and went about their daily lives. But that day their lives would end.

As the plane headed eastward, the bombardier announced the approach to the target, and then the moment when the bomb should be released. Col. Tibbets pulled the switch himself. The new mechanism worked, and the bomb separated from the plane at 26,000 feet.

They turned immediately and flew back toward Tinian. They wanted to be on their way home and as far away from the blast as possible.

Empty of cargo, the *Enola Gay* sped up, reaching its maximum speed of 300 mph. The bomb fell for one minute then detonated in the air at 1,800 feet. While the bomb was plummeting, the plane flew five miles toward home. Because the bomb fell almost straight down, the *Enola Gay* was six miles away from the blast. At that distance, the blast wind reached them, but it would have slowed from its original 900 mph to only a little more than the speed of the plane. They almost outran it.

It was 8:15 a.m.

The cabin of the airplane lit up as if there were a second sun. Fifteen seconds later the plane was buffeted by two bumps from the rear. It was the blast wind, but it wasn't serious. The pilot turned the plane back toward the city to get a look at what they had done. The mushroom cloud was already as high as they were and climbing.

On the ground, people had been going to work, exercising, just finishing breakfast. Seventy thousand of them died instantly from the blast wind. Later more died from burns and radiation poisoning. All buildings within 1.5 miles were blown down. It was said that the wind hit the mountains behind the town and then bounced back to hit the town again, but the blast wind would not have behaved like this. It was the shock wave, not unlike a sound wave, traveling at 1,100 feet per second, that bounced off the mountains. It preceded the wind.

From the Enola Gay, the flight crew saw fires everywhere on the ground. It was the biggest bomb they had ever seen, and no one would see another one exploded in combat for a long time, except of course for the one being dropped at nearly the same time on Nagasaki. But that one did not create as much damage as the one in Hiroshima.

The heat was also intense. On the ground, beneath the explosion, the temperature was about 7,000 degrees, hot enough to melt metals and vaporize the more fragile bodies of people, plants, and animals. Even concrete surfaces were damaged. In several places there were nuclear "shadows" where the damage done to stone and concrete structures was less because human or plant life in front of it had absorbed some of the energy. Ceramic tiles close to the center of the blast area melted. People who were over a mile away had the clothes they were wearing catch fire.

Radiation burns and other problems came later. Many women who were pregnant aborted. Later less lucky babies were born with deformities. The aftereffects of the radiation lasted for years. By the end of the first year, more than 140,000 people had died. Those who died later from radiation exposure increased this number to nearly 200,000.

The Enola Gay returned to base. It is not certain what the crew felt — surely some elation at the success of a mission they knew to be very important. Their initial reactions, however, suggest they also felt some remorse, even right after *the blast when they had only an inkling of the full extent of the damage. But feelings of remorse would surely have been countered by the anger virtually all Americans felt toward the Japanese. Maybe the men also felt some hope that the war would be brought to a more rapid end by their action. In any event, they would soon realize their mission had just that effect, although at a horrible cost. American lives were no doubt saved by the speedy surrender that followed, but many innocent Japanese lives were lost too. The men who flew the Enola Gay were heroes to many — it was a dangerous mission, which they undertook with great bravery — but they were also villains to many others. It was surely impossible then, and difficult even today, to find a middle position between these two extremes.*

The bomb they were carrying was codenamed Little Boy.

The Little Boy wasn't very little. It was 10 feet long, a couple of feet wide, and weighed four and a half tons. It contained 60 kilograms of uranium-235, which had been "enriched" to make it fissionable. Less than one kilogram, however, underwent fission. The design was called a "gun barrel," in which a regular explosive charge was ignited behind one chunk of uranium, sending it like a bullet down a steel tube, where it collided with another chunk of the same material, starting the fission or chain reaction. As soon as the chain reaction began, with atoms splitting and shooting off subatomic particles to break up other atoms, the explosion tore open the bomb casing so that the uranium was no longer contained, and then the chain reaction stopped. Nevertheless, the fission of less than one kilogram of the material was equal to 13,000 tons of TNT and, with the bomb that fell on Nagasaki three days later, brought an end to the war in the Pacific.

The Little Boy had one drawback — a severe bump during transport could cause the "bullet" to be fired accidentally down the "gun barrel" and initiate the chain reaction. It was consequently dangerous to transport the bomb. Had the Enola Gay been forced to ditch in the Pacific, for example, a nuclear explosion could have resulted.

14. THE DOSSIERS

Monday, Late Afternoon. New York City

By the time I get back to my office, I'm eager to talk to Jim and get approval for my atom bomb story. But no. Not yet. A guy is sitting in the chair next to my computer. Dark suit. Short hair. I'm not surprised when he says, "I've got an envelope from Tom Shipman." Those FBI guys must have a dress code.

With a little nod, he hands me a fat envelope, which somehow tells me what's in the envelope is important. I'm pretty sure it's not a love note.

"Thanks," I say. "And say thanks to Tom for me."

He doesn't respond to that. Just turns on his heel and walks away. I open the envelope and see it has two dossiers for me to read.

The first one is the woman's, and she's the one I'm most interested in. I've worked out in my head what might motivate the radical Muslim guys to kill people, but I have trouble understanding how a young woman brought up in America could want to join a terrorist cell and blow up part of her own country.

The heading on the first page is "Gretchen Harris." That's her real name. Ouch. Why did her parents name her Gretchen? She started out with a strike against her. Her story, however, is fascinating. She ran away at 13 from her home in Salt Lake City. Her parents were religious, at least on the outside, regular churchgoers. But as we all know, churchgoing doth not always a good person make. The mother had been treated at the hospital a couple of times for multiple bruises and once for a broken cheekbone. She'd refused to name her husband as the assailant, saying instead it was a black man who had come at her "out of nowhere." The officer writing the report lets his sarcasm show here and there. It was obvious to him the husband had beaten her. The girl was 11 at the time, and I could only guess what effect seeing her father beat up her mother would have had.

At 13 she too shows up in the hospital records, but this time she's the patient, and the complaints are not recorded. Obviously it's something sensitive enough to be kept confidential. But the police went to her house and talked to the father, although the police record doesn't say what it was all about. Again it isn't hard to read between the lines. It looks to me as though the authorities are conspiring to keep the father's name out of the record as a child abuser. From my point of view, it doesn't matter; the guy was doing it to his daughter. I know it happens all the time, but it's still despicable.

A few weeks later she ran.

After she ran away, a lot of time passes — blanks in the record. She shows up in New York nearly a year later, picked up for soliciting in Times Square. My guess is she turned tricks in cities across the country, working her way east, probably getting into and out of the clutches of different pimps.

Then for another five years, there's nothing in the record. She applies to have her name legally changed. Probably something good came into her life. Maybe a guy. Maybe she found religion, and maybe that religion was Islam. Whatever it was saved her life, but didn't take away the hatred. In the end she got recruited by a terrorist organization.

The dossier gave some answers, but it also raises questions. If I ever get a chance to write this story up, the background story of Gretchen Harris, aka Becca Jordan, will bring insight.

The second dossier is called "Toby Williams," aka Nathaniel.

Nat's parents are wealthy Iowa farmers who raise corn and feed it to cattle. At least that's the plan. The reality is a little different. According to the bank records, the family's one of the richest in the state, and their income is more than three-quarters from the Federal Government.

The Williams are rich all right, but they do it by collecting subsidies, payments to keep production high and prices low. Consumers benefit, but smaller farmers are squeezed out.

Toby went to the local public high school, which had high standards and good teachers. From his pioneering ancestors, he inherited a streak of idealism and the belief that few things are more virtuous than hard work. So his stomach churned when he discovered his father's money came mostly from subsidies. He felt all the talk he'd heard from his father about the independence and romance of being a rancher was bullshit. He wasn't a rancher; the only thing he rounded up were government checks. The cattle were just show-paraded in front of the IRS to justify the subsidy money.

At the local community college, he discovered the subsidies his father received made farmers in Africa unable to make money raising cattle. His family's wealth caused the starvation of African babies. How could he sit down at the dinner table and eat a steak? He tried to talk to his father about it, but he got a lecture about the American way, and the importance of hard work.

But the more he learned, the more he thought his father's way *wasn't* the American way, that enterprise wasn't free if it depended on government help, and ruined farmers in other countries. Was it really such hard work to endorse checks?

He was disgusted at the whole business, and one day, after a big fight with his father, he stormed out of the house and drove off in his late-model SUV. In New York he sold his car and found laboring jobs and felt good working at them. It was honesty he craved — the dollars he made came from the blisters on his hands.

But in New York too, he saw rampant greed. Stock market investors didn't really work. The actors and dancers on Broadway made their fortunes by entertaining only the wealthy. Everywhere he saw corruption.

One day on a lunch break at a construction site, he was spouting some of these ideas to his fellow workers when a Muslim coworker suggested he might want to go to a mosque, which he did. There he found people who believed the spiritual side of life was more important and wanted to reinstate values in the world through Islam. The asceticism and fire of religious fervor found a place in him, fed by the hatred he felt toward the smug farmers he had known at home. He was easy for the terrorists to recruit.

The stories of Nat and Becca made me wonder how many other idealistic young people are turned off by the inequities they see around them. And as I think about their lives, I can't help but admire the investigative work that goes into compiling a dossier. Someone had to ask hundreds of questions and read pages of lists and forms and reports before a story like this — revealing the motivations of the subject — could be compiled.

It's nearly 6 p.m., and my Col. Haldane story needs to get out. I sit down and make little keyboarding movements with both hands in the air poised just above the keys, as if I were warming up for the typing Olympics. Then I ceremoniously lower my fingers and touch the keys to initiate the process. The terminal awakes from electronic slumber. I don't understand how it does that. I love it.

But all those thoughts settling into my head on the train have flown off. The danger to the country is so big, the greed of the VP's guys so blatant, that the story simply doesn't ring true. It sounds too overdrawn. Too much for the average reader to comprehend.

Process B to the rescue. Sometimes I figure out how to handle a story while I'm asleep. I'll go to bed unsure, troubled, unable to figure out how to write a story, and when I wake up in the morning, it's all there in my head, ready and waiting for me to set it down, as if I'd ordered it like a pizza for home delivery. When I get ideas in this way, I feel as if they've been given to me, provided by a bountiful universe, an answer to prayer, as if I were a shaman seeking guidance from the Great Spirit, and having fasted alone in a cave in the wilderness, the stars or the trees or the wind have spoken to me and revealed the truth. So I pack my things and head home, eager to see if a night's sleep will give me the answers.

I almost forget that Gaylord, his dweeby friend, and I bugged the Jordans' apartment, and I'm suddenly eager to hear if the new system has recorded anything of interest. It's nearly 8 p.m. when I switch on the recording device and hear almost nothing. The room bug has activated the recorder twice as a result of shouts from the street. Of course, the Jordans aren't home during the day. The computer too is silent.

Then they come home. She comes in first, and I can hear her muttering to herself about the mail then finding her jogging outfit. While she's changing, he comes in and they say a few words about dinner. He's going to cook. Big deal. I almost regret spending my money on this equipment. It's just boring.

I listen to them until 11:00, when they go to bed. There's just nothing interesting, although I confess to the guilty pleasure of listening in on someone else's domestic life. That pleasure would be enough for me if they gave any indication they were romantically interested in each other. But that possibility is a dead end, it seems. So I go to bed too.

15. AN ANOMALY AT SEA

The sun rises suddenly, as it always seems to do at sea. Captain Zhakdin watches it intensely, noting the changes in the cloud color, the altered angles of the sun's rays, and the deepening of the ocean's blue. He enjoys many things about his job, but none more than this — seeing first-hand the things he could only dream about as a child in Issyk. There, the nearest ocean was several thousand miles away, so distant as to be not quite real, a place found only in the imagination and therefore magical. Now he lives in this magical world, and it is, if anything, more wonderful than he imagined. He cannot take his eyes off it.

The captain read in his youth about sunrises at sea, about the vividness of the colors, the sensation of feeling the earth's roundness, and the shock of bright sunlight coming only seconds after the first rays. And reading he had pictured these things. As a child he imagined the sun, an orange ball, popping up out of the water like a bright frog in a vast pond. And now he greets the sun. At the end of the day, he will watch the sun go down so fast he can almost hear it falling into the water. And sometimes there is that eerie green flash. He often lingers on the bridge just to see the sunset, imagining the plop.

Today there is a slight swell, four-foot waves moving steadily southward, the gentle remnants of yesterday's storm. He knows now from his university studies why the waves always move at the same speed, and knowing has not diminished the magic of it. The ship is not rolling so badly now, and the galley crew has brought the captain's morning tea to the bridge in two ordinary pots. They are more home-like than the heavy-weather pots clamped to the tray with covers fastened down against spillage. The captain appreciates the difference. In the Kazakh tradition, one pot is for extra-strong black tea, another for hot water, with milk and sugar on the side, prepared just as he has instructed the galley. On the tray too is the captain's austere breakfast — two slices of dark bread smeared with butter. Captain Zhakdin takes in no more calories than he needs to maintain his current trim, and he works out regularly in the paltry little gym room below decks.

The nearly horizontal rays shine through the glass of the bridge window and reach the small glass pot containing the strong black tea, revealing an amber core. Captain Zhakdin smiles at the thought of sunlight finding kinship in dark tea. He sighs with deep contentment as he pours no more than a few tablespoons of the bitter brew into the bottom of the traditionally handleless Kazakh cup — a gift from his mother at his last parting from her now more than a year ago. He writes to her regularly, as well as to his three sisters whom he deviled mercilessly when, as the only boy in a Kazakh household, he was treated not quite as a king, but certainly better than a prince. He misses them, but he is too happy and excited, yes, still excited, to be in this job that allows him to live most of his days on his beloved ocean.

He adds milk to his tea, sips it with great pleasure, holding the cup with his thumb and middle finger on the sides and his index finger on the inside for stability. He enjoys the feeling of warmth on his fingers. As he munches his meager breakfast, the sun, pouring through the glass walls of the bridge, warms his body.

Far off to one side of the ship's bow, a group of dolphins play. They look as happy as Captain Zhakdin feels. He looks aft. Behind the ship a half dozen seagulls soar, sporting in the gentle air currents caused by the passage of his ship's superstructure.

The weather is excellent, and the forecasting service on the

Internet suggests the good weather will continue for the rest of his crossing to Elizabeth, NJ, where he will unload his entire cargo and then take on another full load of containers bound for a series of ports in Spain and Italy. After that he will take his ship through the Mediterranean to Cairo, Tel Aviv, and Nicosia, and then up the Bosporus to southern Russian ports in the Black Sea. There, he is planning to have his wife travel to visit him, while his ship undergoes some refitting.

He orders the first mate to run the check on the containers. The system is new, designed after the terrorist attacks on the U.S. that brought down the World Trade Center buildings in New York City, to the surprise, shock, and horror of the rest of the world, including Russia. The new system was installed only recently after many bureaucratic delays and has been used only once before. Even now there are many containers that have not been fitted with the internal device that permits a check on their contents while the ship is at sea. The containers that have passed through the U.S. and the European countries, however, have already been fitted with these small devices that communicate with the on-board computer.

The first mate nods his compliance and heads for the computer room, in the first level below the main deck. He sits down at his workstation and brings up the program, which presents on the screen a list of all the containers in the "stack," each labeled by its position in the tier, column, and row. One at a time, he places his cursor on the entry and clicks on the "run analysis" button. For those containers outfitted with the analyzer / transponder (AT), the computer sends out a small radio signal, telling the AT to scan the contents of the box.

In less than a second, it returns with a list of the electronic labels, showing the point of origin (the TCO, his company's name, telephone number, city, and country), the contents, and dimensions of the carton, and its value and Customs status. It does not analyze the container for density or radioactivity, the two pieces of information that would clearly show a weighty, highly radioactive object in the center of the dirty yellow container, exactly the information that would lead one to suspect a nuclear device. Both density and radioactivity need to be assessed because terrorists might surround the bomb with lead to hide the radioactivity. This would hide the radioactivity but increase the density of the object.

The analysis of the dirty yellow container shows numerous cartons of cosmetics. However, from the dimensions of each carton, the total space taken up by the cargo within the container, the analysis shows that inside the container located in tier three, row three, cross-array four, there is some space unaccounted for by the summed dimensions of the cartons of cosmetics.

The anomaly is not something the first mate has seen before. In fact he has run only one of these analyses previously because the system is so new. The anomaly seems unusual enough to report to the captain, so after performing the on-board computer analysis on all the containers, he prints out the result, pencils in a little star in the margin of the printout, folds it up, and puts it in his shirt pocket before exiting the program and turning off the computer. Then he heads for the bridge.

"*Kapitein*," the first mate says in flawless Russian as he enters the bridge, "there is a peculiar result in the analysis of one of the containers."

"I see, let me see the report," the captain answers in Russian strongly accented by a childhood on the Steppe. The first mate is careful not to smile. The captain's accent reminds him of shepherds and camel drivers, rather than seagoing discipline, but he is no fool. Nothing shows on his face as he hands the report to his superior officer.

"I have marked it with a star in the margin."

"I see, hmmm, yes, some space is unaccounted for. And the container is located, yes, in the middle of the stack. Is there room in the hold to shift the containers off the top of it?"

The captain knows that, in fact, there is enough room to do this, but he often enjoys asking these questions as a kind of test of his crew.

"Yes, there is room in the hold, but the cargo crew is still sleeping. I have let them sleep late because of the storm last night."

"Of course, let them sleep. No one slept well last night."

"Yes, *Kapitein*." The mate then returns to his regular station without a clear idea of what to do about the odd space. It is probable, indeed most likely, the container is just not fully loaded, although to leave space in a container is wasteful because the cost of shipping is the same regardless of the load in it. Few shippers would leave space unoccupied, unless of course their manufacturing process had been balked in some way, and they simply did not have enough product to complete the load in time to catch the ship's departure. There are probably many such explanations, and the mate does not consider the situation a serious problem as he stuffs the report into his shirt and goes down to the wardroom on the lower deck for his breakfast.

The captain also thinks the anomaly is probably unimportant. According to the protocols he has read attached to the contract between the ship's owners and the American shipping companies, he is supposed to investigate these anomalies. But to activate the crane, hoist containers up out of a tier twice, placing them temporarily on top of the fifth tier then plucking the suspicious container out of its location on the third tier and lowering it to the deck where the crew can open it and inspect the contents, would occupy his crew for a considerable period of time, and he would prefer they be alert and rested when the ship reaches port in Elizabeth. He decides to wait until the men have had some extra rest, then he will figure out what to do about the odd container.

On Wednesday, however, after the crew has finished repairing many of the minor problems caused by Monday's storm, a large bolt, weakened by the storm, shears off and falls into a crack between the hull and an area below the deck used as a conduit for electrical wires. The bolt is heavy, and it tears through one of the wires, producing a short circuit that shuts down the ship's electronics. Alarms sound. In the darkened engine room, men grope for the emergency generator switches, which bring on the dim emergency lights. On the bridge the captain hears nothing but silence when he picks up the telephone to ask the engine room for a report, and he has to come down from the bridge to inspect the difficulty. Engine number three had begun to vibrate unusually just as the lights went out, so the engine was turned off, slowing the ship, and the crew, joined soon by the captain himself, concentrate their investigation in the area around engine number three.

In a few minutes, they find the massive flange knocking against the hull as the ship rolls in the swell. One of the huge bolts is missing. From that it is easy enough to look down into the conduit area and see where the heavy piece of metal has fallen. They fish it out with a broomstick and a long piece of wire. That is the easy part. Then they have to repair the electrical break. To do so they open the conduit from below which means going into the crawl space below the engine compartment, pulling the broken wire out from both ends, and then running a new wire in along the length of the conduit, and reconnecting it to the terminals at either end. This part of the repair takes the ship's electrician several hours. The captain, the first mate, and several specialist members of the crew also participate, but eventually the lights come back on, and cheering is heard throughout the ship.

The first mate was the one to reach deep into the conduit and pull one end of the wire through, and in doing so the right sleeve of his shirt became filthy with grease and soot. The laundry room is on the way to his cabin, so he strips off his shirt and leaves it there as he goes by. He is tired and falls into his bunk for a short nap. The report of the on-board analysis goes into the giant washing machine and is reduced to pulp. Dealing with the electrical emergency has, in a very similar way, washed from his memory the anomalous container report. In time he will remember it, but by then it will be too late.

16. THE STORY EMERGES

Tuesday. New York

When I get up the next morning, I don't have the flash of inspiration on Col. Haldane's story I'd hoped for, and I set it aside while I listen to the Jordans for a while. Monosyllabic morning mutterings, as I call them, feeling alliterative, fill their morning. When they've both left for work, I turn on my laptop to work a little while I have another cup of coffee. There on the screen is a report labeled "Mr. Jordan's recent computer activity."

Nat had been going through his email, and they're all foreign sources, mostly Middle Eastern locations. Those last two little letters at the end of the email addresses give that away. But the content is hard to figure out. Mostly it's odd reports of family affairs — Cousin Yasimeen is getting married, an aunt is ill. That kind of thing. But after a while, I realize the messages are a little more disconnected than they should be, and I begin to suspect they're coded.

One of them is particularly intriguing. It reads "Michael Jordan says the team is buying new sneakers, and they don't have those special laces." I think about who or what "Michael Jordan" might be. I can't tell. Nat answered the message about the sneakers in a congratulatory tone that seems out of place. I wonder if they're talking about the container ship devices. When I take another look at the incoming message about "Michael Jordan," I notice the guy sending it from Riyadh has left the message "Michael Jordan" attached, and it has a "pentagon. gov/procure" suffix. Obviously, the message about Michael had come from the Pentagon, and that means there's a mole in the procurement office.

I call Col. Haldane right away. I don't even have time to enjoy Edward's voice.

"I have something important for you."

"I'll call you back."

Ten minutes later, my landline rings; it's Col. Haldane.

"What is it?" She sounds serious, as if she knows this must be something important, which it is.

I give her all the details and let her come to her own conclusion.

"We have a mole in procurement."

"That's what I thought too."

"I've suspected it for quite a long time, but I always assumed it was one of the VP's spies. Now I see it's more serious than that."

"Yes, ma'am." I don't know what the appropriate response is. It's hard to imagine anything more serious than a corrupt vice president.

"I have to think carefully about what to do. I don't have much credibility in the department right now."

"Maybe you should go to another agency." My suggestion seems feeble.

"Of course, but which one? I'll have to think about it. Kimmie, thank you. Keep listening on your devices, and let me know if anything else interesting comes up."

"I'll do that."

Then she adds, "I've got something for you too."

"Go ahead."

"Remember at the luncheonette I said I didn't know when Bentley's container inspection device had been approved?"

"Yes."

"It's worse than I imagined. It was approved secretly three months ago. The whole effort to request bids and evaluate them was a complete sham. In fact the devices have already been installed in most of the containers that come to the U.S."

"It seems really fast."

"It's too goddamned fast," she says angrily.

"It means they wanted to create a fait accompli so they've made their money before anyone starts an investigation."

"But you said the investigations didn't matter because they had the votes to keep them from getting to the floor." I want to believe her, but there's a discrepancy, and I have to check it out.

"Yes. That's right. They don't care about the investigations finding them guilty. But when a product the army's using is under investigation, we stop using it. The investigation would have slowed the sale, so they kept it under wraps."

"Shit." I try not to swear too much, but this seems like the right kind of occasion.

"Exactly."

"I don't know when I'm going to get a chance to write this one up; a lot's going on right now."

"You got that right." After that we say our goodbyes and hang up.

I sit back in my chair and let a huge sigh fall out of my lungs. I've got my story.

***

First, I call Tom and tell him about the mole. I'll need backup, someone who knows what I'm working on.

"Is there anything I can do to help?"

"No. I just need someone else to hear the story."

"Kimmie, I should probably report this to someone in the Homeland Security Office, or somewhere official." I wonder why he adds that "or" clause. To me, HSO seems like exactly the right place to report it. My reporter's ears, however, picked up on some hesitation in his mind.

"I know that. I want you to. It'll help Colonel Haldane be taken seriously."

"Yes, it will."

"You'll keep me out of it?" I don't want government types breathing down my neck just now.

"Absolutely." And I know I'm going to be all right.

I don't tell him about the second half of my conversation with the colonel, about the secret sale and the sham bidding. He's got enough on his mind. After we hang up, I wonder why he said he was "probably" going to report it.

Then I get to work and write the story. It takes an hour to produce the first draft then another hour to go through it painstakingly to make sure it's worded as carefully as possible. I'm not crazy about it. It seems a little too cut and dried for the material. There should be more anger, more outrage. But I'm writing a news story, not an editorial. I email it to Jim. He reads it right away, and I get the answer back in ten minutes.

"Page two, tomorrow." He doesn't need to say more.

Then I send a copy of the story to one of our editorial writers, hoping he'll write something that conveys the outrage.

17. THE ATTORNEY GENERAL'S OFFICE

Tuesday. Washington, D.C.

The attorney general of the United States occupies an appropriately huge office in Washington overlooking the Mall. He sits at a large, custom-made desk with a computer terminal and three telephones. He has numerous aides, the best legal minds that can be persuaded to work for the administration, and three secretarial assistants who make sure appointments are kept and paperwork is generated on time and filed in a coherent system. These ancillary individuals come and go often. The AG flourishes amid all the activity; his solemn yet hurried words bear on important matters of the law, of threats to the nation, and of the political winds that blow strongly in Washington.

The attorney general is an old friend of the president's — they were fraternity brothers in college. Both then went on to different law schools. The president went to one of the most prestigious law schools in the country and did poorly. But he had good family connections, and it was rumored he scraped through law school on the strength of them. The AG, on the other hand, did not have any connections and knew perfectly well he was not a brilliant student. He chose a middle-sized city with a new law school, opened two years before in a mediocre university. They were eager to get him, and he finished in the middle of his class. His is not a brilliant legal mind, but that is OK; aides are paid to be brilliant. The AG has a more important quality — his loyalty to the president. Legal shenanigans are common in Washington, and this administration has more than its share. The president foresees the day when it will be useful for the chief law enforcement officer of the country to be a friend.

The attorney general receives a memo by email from Col. Haldane about the mole. He prints it out and reads the paper copy. He shakes his head slowly in disbelief then sends the electronic copy to his assistant, who reads it in about one-quarter of the time.

The assistant finishes reading, walks into his boss' office, holds the paper ostentatiously over the wastebasket, and looks inquisitively at his boss.

"She will do anything," the AG says then nods, and the assistant releases the printout, which floats down toward the antique wicker wastebasket but sails to one side on the room's stale air and misses the basket. The assistant curses, picks it up, and angrily stuffs it in the basket. The AG, however, does not delete the email.

Later the same day, after a call from a Tom Shipman at the FBI, the AG rereads the email from Col. Haldane, and then calls in the FBI director. The director was appointed by the previous administration and has held on to his job because he was the first fully competent director the FBI had seen in a long time. He knows how to use public opinion and is very popular with the people, so the new president had no choice but to keep him on.

The AG greets him perfunctorily and gestures for the director to sit, but he remains standing.

"Do you know about this?" the AG asks, holding the Haldane memo between his thumb and index finger while he waves it slowly back and forth.

"Yes, sir. I am familiar with Colonel Haldane. She has complained previously about the vice president having too much influence over the procurement process."

"I see," the AG says evenly so as not to reveal his animosity toward the colonel.

"Do you believe her story?" the director asks.

Although he is disgusted by Col. Haldane's complaint, which he considers a betrayal of trust from a snotty, holier-than-thou female, the AG knows quite well that she is correct and is about to blow up an arrangement that he has benefitted from.

"Yes, I do," he answers after a brief pause in which he sees the handwriting on the wall.

And the handwriting is easy to read —it is time to see the vice president in a different light. An investigation is likely, and the AG knows the outcome: Bentley will be found guilty. He turns the question back to the director, a debating trick he learned in college.

"Will there be an investigation?" he asks.

"Yes. Of course."

"Is she credible?"

"Yes. She has a good record, has always been a very straight shooter, not the type to do something out of revenge. She is a good soldier. Our Manhattan office has the same information, although the agent will not tell me his source. I have to act on it."

"I understand," the attorney general says somewhat sadly. He knows there will be changes around Washington. He realizes he will have to roll with the punches like everyone else. But before rolling, he will call the president to warn him of the obvious political consequences.

After the director leaves, he makes the call to the Oval Office.

"Mr. President, there is a Colonel Haldane in the Pentagon,

who…"

"Yes. I know. I read the article. There is no need to do anything," the president says.

"In time, you will…"

"Sure, in time. And when the time comes, I can cut bait." He does not need to act yet at all.

"Sure. I get it," the AG responds vaguely, covering up his ignorance about the fishing reference.

***

The AG calls the vice president's office and tells one of the VP's staff officers Col. Haldane's story is being reported in the press.

The vice president's aide — Jon Matson — hangs up the phone and calls in one of his associates.

"You know the story about Colonel Haldane." He says this with more authority than he has.

"Yeah, the one that bitch at the *Times* wrote."

"That's the one. She's found out something she shouldn't know about."

"Who's her source?"

Matson looks at him contemptuously. "Who do you think?"

"It could be the colonel." The aide is suddenly unsure of himself.

"Of course it's the colonel, you idiot. Who else could it be?"

"I don't know, maybe…"

"It's the colonel." Matson cuts him off.

"Can we…"

"No we can't. Haven't you got any sense at all? Colonel Haldane looks like a victim in these stories. We know she's obstructing the defense of her country, but the *Times* bitch makes her look like a hero."

"So, if we do something to make her keep quiet…"

"Brilliant conclusion," Matson says sarcastically. "'No shit, Sherlock,' we used to say."

"So, what do you suggest?"

"What I *suggest*..." Matson emphasizes the word so the aide will understand it's not a suggestion but an order, "is we arrange for Miss *Times* Bitch to have an accident, preferably one that will end her writing career."

"OK. I can arrange that."

"You're damned right you can. That's why you're on my staff. It's not because of your brain."

"Yes, sir."

18. THE WARNING

Wednesday. New York City

The next morning, my story breaks, front page. And the editorial staff didn't let me down. For a reporter, there's no thrill like seeing your own story in print. And for me, a story that uncovers skullduggery at the highest levels of government is the best of all. I celebrate by getting breakfast at the coffee shop. This time, it'll be my neighborhood corner coffee shop.

Outside, the temperature is friendly. It's only a short walk to the coffee shop anyway. As I walk past New Yorkers on their way to work, and those few coming home after a night shift, I have that feeling — it's hard to describe — when you've done something special or something wonderful has happened to you, but the people around you are strangers who don't know about your good fortune. They don't share in your happiness. I've felt this before — a secret gloating, I guess. Probably, they wouldn't even be interested, and they'd certainly dismiss me if I started talking about it, but there's a small temptation to do that, to tell people. It's harder to have good news and not share it than bad news. Bad news you can keep to yourself. And yet the newspapers, those giant systems for disseminating information, hardly ever tell good news. People seem more interested in the tragedies of their fellow citizens. The fires and murders and industrial accidents are news; they sell papers. So do the political scandals, the tumbling down — and sometimes breaking — of our political Humpty Dumpties. But good news is rarely reported. A paper focused on good news would surely fold.

Lost in philosophical ramblings about news and politics, I almost miss my breakfast place. I'm hungry. Just walking inside and smelling the aroma has me salivating. I love New York's coffee shops. Some people call them luncheonettes, but the word is misleading. Most of them are open and crowded at breakfast. And they should be. Their breakfasts are spectacular. The one I found on 84th is a little more upscale than most. In New York a restaurant is upscale when the wait staff is pleasant. And the food in these places is wonderful. I order lox and bagels, which comes on a platter the size of a small aircraft carrier and has, as a garnish to the lox and bagels, a whole 4-ounce packet of Philadelphia cream cheese, fresh lettuce and tomatoes, rings of red onions, and Spanish capers dribbled over the whole thing. The bagel is toasted, and the lox is mild and smoky, sliced as thin as paper and draped with loving care over the two bagel halves. It's a breakfast that would have made Henry VIII burp, but he probably didn't know about bagels and lox, the poor schlub, and had to make do with a haunch of young doe.

I buy a *Times* and reread my story while I'm eating. It makes everything taste a little better and removes any guilt I may feel about the permanent damage I'm doing to my figure, liver, cardiovascular system, and fingernails. Fingernails? Well the way I use them to tear into the toasted bagels causes a little breakage now and again.

After breakfast I ease myself out of my chair, trying hard not to belch too obviously, tell the waiter he's one of the sexiest men I've ever laid eyes on, and pay my bill, tipping him a little too generously considering the compliment. Then I walk to the nearest bus stop.

The weather's changed. Gray clouds scud past the tops of the buildings, and a sharp wind blows dust and debris in little swirls. I'm glad for the cold. It forces me to walk briskly, which is almost like exercise after the meal I've just had. I grab a downtown bus, one of my personal chariots, and ride staring out the window at all the wonderful people, assuming most of them have read my story. I look around the bus too, and there are a few *Times* spread open then folded into long vertical strips, the way New Yorkers do. The tabloids have to be folded only once. A good paper, like the *Times*, takes a little more effort. I smile to myself.

***

I walk into the office, and Jim motions for me to join him. He's in the shirtsleeves and jeans he inevitably wears, an old hippy — the salt-and-pepper ponytail is a dead giveaway. There are still a lot of these geriatric hippies, now deep in the establishment, even, like Jim, very dedicated. But they still go home and have a few joints and listen to The Stones before going to bed. He has a serious look on his face.

"Kimmie, what's the oldest joke in journalism?"

I love a challenge, but something about the way Jim says this makes me think I don't want to know the answer.

"I don't know — dog bites man?" I suggest. He shakes his head.

"Good guess. No, it's…"

"Wait, I know, it's the good news, bad news jokes."

"Yes." He still looks serious, and I know I'm not going to hear a joke.

"The good news this morning is that your story is terrific. It's gone viral on the Internet. The *Post* has rewritten it. The wires have all taken up parts of it. It's all over the world."

"Great. That's what's supposed to happen." Then I realize there's a bad news part that Jim's waiting to tell me. "OK, so what's the other half?"

"The bad news is, there's likely to be retaliation."

"What d'you mean? Are they going to try to rub me out?" I grin and wiggle my hips a little then strike a pose with one hip out and my hand on it.

"It's not impossible." He grows suddenly more intense. "You may not fully appreciate just how bad these guys are. They're crooks, nothing more. Somehow, through some fluke of democracy, they've gotten into high positions. It's happened before, you know. Remember Agnew?"

"Who?"

He laughs. "He was a petty crook. These guys are big-time crooks." His speech slows with the implications of his words.

"D'you think they would really try to hurt me?" The bagels and cream cheese start to feel heavy.

"I think they care about the money they're making and nothing else. They have no scruples. The only thing stopping them is your status as a journalist and the fact they would be the prime suspects if anything happened to you. Plus, it doesn't hurt that you have some good friends in law enforcement." These words come tumbling out of Jim's mouth so fast it's hard to follow him, and he stares hard at me but with tenderness in his eyes. He really cares about me. I've never heard him talk like that before or look at me like that, and it worries me.

"D'you have any suggestions?" I'm a little late realizing the last thing he said referred to Tom. I give up the I'm-a-little-teapot pose. The situation has darkened.

"Be careful. Don't go out alone if you can help it, particularly at night. If they're going to try to hurt you, they'll hire very ugly people to do it and cover their own asses." He stands up, and I think he's going to come around from behind his desk and hug me, but he hesitates.

"Not too many people know I've moved. That might help."

I see a ray of hope in this, but I'm still worried.

"Yes, it might. Don't tell anyone else."

"Thanks for the warning, Jim. I'm not sure what to do with it, but I'll keep it in mind." I put my hand on the doorknob, about to leave.

"OK. Just be careful. Keep your eyes open. Call your FBI friend. He may have some better ideas." It's my exit cue, and I notice he doesn't turn his eyes back to his desk. He keeps looking at me.

***

Back at my desk, I turn on my monitor to get my email and find 114 unread messages. We all have huge mailbox accounts because sometimes we expect multiple answers to questions we send out, but this is mostly fan mail. I start reading, and I enjoy most of them. There are a few that say I'm un-American and my article will help the terrorists. I expect that kind of political response from about 20 per cent of our readers, so it's no shock. I count the positives and the negatives, and on the whole people are supportive. Then I look closely at the negatives. One of them stands out. It says:

> *Journalists who do not support our leaders should not be allowed to practice their profession. The world would be better off if journalists just reported the news and stopped trying to find dirt everywhere. You cannot justify your existence by bad-mouthing the vice president.*

There's no indication who's written the letter, and I can't even tell where it comes from. There's a veiled threat in the letter, and I forward it to Tom. He emails me back in less than an hour.

> *Hi Kimmie,*
> *I traced it to a computer in the vice president's office.*

The threat was too vague for me to make any kind of case out of it. But be careful. They are powerful people and wouldn't hesitate to deal with you harshly if they can get away with it. And they probably think they can.

Two people have now told me to "be careful." I wish they'd be more specific. I'm always "careful." I wear galoshes in the winter even though it makes me look like an Iowa pig farmerette. I look both ways. Usually I watch my diet, but not always, like this morning. But how am I supposed to "be careful" to make sure someone doesn't try to kill me? Or if they try, how do I keep them from succeeding? I'm baffled. My confusion doesn't help solve the problem.

***

Later in the afternoon, one of our cub reporters calls in a story from the Village. I read it quickly. Someone has blown up my old apartment, and the explosion sets fire to the building. The NY Fire Department is there quickly, as they usually are, and no one is hurt. The reporter knew it was my old address from a party I gave for my fellow scribblers the previous year.

"Would it be OK, Ms. Hansen, to report it may have been an unsuccessful attempt on your life in retaliation for your story?"

"You can write that, if you want. It won't change anything for me, but it might make *you* a little vulnerable."

"I don't care. That's what we're supposed to do, isn't it?"

"Yup." I nod with the phone in my hand. "That's what we're supposed to do. It says so right there in the Constitution. It just doesn't say much about the consequences."

"Thanks, Ms. Hansen." And I know he's going to write a hell of a story. It's a big break for him to land a story that has national implications. I hope Jim lets him keep it. But I wish the reporter hadn't called me Ms. He must see me on the other side of a generational divide. I hang up the phone and go straight into the ladies' room to look in the mirror. Nothing's changed. I still look pretty good, I think. Then one of the new girls comes in. She's wearing low-cut jeans, and when she leans over the sink they pull tight around her hips. There's no fat on those hips, and at the base of her spine there's a little daisy tattoo, calling attention to the little hollow there. Well, I think, looking in the mirror again, the competition is tougher than it used to be, but maybe experience counts for something. I may not have a tattoo, but I know how to move that part of my body so a man will look at it. "I don't need no fucking tattoo," I say under my breath to the mirror. I finish up and hurry out. Bravado helps.

I take the train home. It's faster, and I feel less conspicuous, but it isn't as entertaining. The people are less friendly on the trains. They push a little harder to get through the doors before they close. And once on, they read or stare grimly at the ads. They don't look at each other. These trains are underground and are properly called subways, but New Yorkers always call them "trains." A person who calls them "subways" is either a newcomer or a tourist.

I think about being in danger and the nastiness of the people I wrote about, and I find no joy in looking at my fellow passengers, so I'm glad to get off the train and up onto the street. I hurry toward home thinking about safety and security.

I'm so preoccupied with all this bad stuff I almost forget to look up as I turn the corner to my block. When I do, I see there's a flowerpot in the Jordan's apartment window that wasn't there before. I stop dead in my tracks and stand there looking at it for a few seconds. It's right in the middle of the windowsill. It's an ordinary, salmon-colored flowerpot with a single red flower in it, probably a fake geranium. I'm sure it's a signal. Suddenly I want to listen to my recorders.

I come into my apartment cautiously, wondering if someone's been there. I go first into the bathroom and examine the tub and sink and the toilet. I don't know why, except it's my private space, and I don't want bad guys in it. Everything's OK and apparently unused. Then I look in my medicine cabinet to see if someone's put something in my aspirin bottle. I'm lucky and don't have a lot of stuff. I even look at my toothpaste. Everything looks OK. Then I check out the kitchen. There are a lot of ways someone could put something in my food. There's an open carton of milk in the refrigerator, which I throw out, and an unopened container of yogurt, which I examine very carefully for punctures. I look over everything in the whole apartment but find no sign anyone's been there. It bothers me that I have to think like this. Life didn't used to be so complicated.

I check the listening devices. There's the usual brief, meaningless stuff on the cell phones. Twice the voice activation goes on because of a noise in the street or a thump from the apartment upstairs, then it turns off. I turn on my computer and find "Mr. Jordan has received and deleted three new messages." All three are reproduced on my screen. They're all like those earlier ones — short and disconnected:

Oct. 20 — Hello Becca: Hakim says the university is harder than he thought it would be. Suleiman.

Oct. 20 — Hi Nat: The *Malchik* is on his way. Arrival details to follow. Suleiman.

Oct. 20 — Dear Becca: Aunt Zaira wants you to remember to dress warmly. Winter is coming, and it is cold where you are. Suleiman.

That doesn't mean too much as far as I can tell. The only odd thing is the word *Malchik*, which sounds more Slavic than Arabic. I find a Russian language dictionary on the Internet and look it up. Everything's in the Cyrillic alphabet, where P is R and C is S. I'm about to give up when I find a site that prints Russian in English letters, and I look the word up. "Little boy," it says. My heart starts to beat faster. I wonder if it could be what it sounds like — a nuclear device of the kind Col. Haldane described. She said they were called Little Boy. My heart is beating hard, and I feel the hair on the back of my neck stand up too, and my palms start to sweat.

I call Tom. He answers on the second ring.

"Hi, Kimmie. What's up in poshville?"

"I think something big is up."

"Tell me."

I tell him about the *Malchik* message, buried but ineffectively, among other messages.

"Yeah, it could mean something."

"Does it mean what I think it means?"

"Yeah, that's what it sounds like."

"What should we do?"

"I'm thinking."

"Shouldn't we call Homeland Security?"

"Not necessarily."

"Why not?"

"I'll explain that to you at some other time, I think. For now, you keep monitoring that apartment. I have to talk to my boss."

"OK. Well, that makes sense anyway."

"After I speak to the director, I want to come over and listen with you."

That sounds encouraging to me, on the romantic front. We'll be listening together. It's not a romantic setting, considering what we'll be listening for, but it's some time alone together.

"OK. Come on over. I'll be here."

We hang up. Tom, of course, doesn't say goodbye.

19. THE PLANS

Wednesday. New York City

I sit at my window and wait, watching the street to find out what the signal means. Does it indicate a meeting has been called? What else could it mean? And if there's a meeting, will all of them come or just some? My receiver's turned on, and domestic sounds come from the Jordans' apartment — dishes rattling, eating sounds, water splashing as they clean up.

Why don't they talk? Are they together just to do a job? Still, why no chit-chat? In the same situation, I wouldn't act that way. I've been thrown together with guys on assignment, and we always ended up friends. Sometimes more. Sure, plotting New York City's destruction might infect a developing relationship. It'd be hard to goof around or fall in love if you're the instrument of death for thousands, maybe millions, of innocent people. Despite the enormity, it doesn't seem like a good explanation. Perhaps these two people absolutely hate each other. Something in their history — a previous relationship or something more sinister – might grow hate. It could be useful, I think, to know more about their relationship. We could exploit it.

I watch for Tom too as I sit by the window. Is this business? Or maybe he wants to come over anyway, and listening was a good excuse. Maybe he just wants to see me.

At 4:30 the two brothers come around the corner together, headed home. One of them looks up then stops and points at the flowerpot. Then they both hurry into their building across the street. That settles it; the flowerpot is a signal.

The other two come in separately. First Muhammad at

about 5:15. He looks up and sees the signal, hesitates slightly, then nods as if to acknowledge receiving the message. Al comes in last at 5:35, and I see him look up, but he doesn't break stride or show any other reaction. Al is very cool.

Nothing happens for an hour. They're all chowing down, I guess. At 6:30 sharp all four emerge simultaneously from their two apartment buildings and cross the street, disappearing below into my building. Their precision is impressive. Tom comes about five minutes later. I feel my heart speed up as I buzz him in.

"You just missed the gathering of the clans," I say as he comes in the door. He gives me a disappointing little peck on the cheek. We have work to do.

We go into the living room where the receiver is, stand expectantly on either side of it, and keep quiet. The recorder is wired directly to the receiver so noises we make won't be recorded, but we don't want to miss anything.

Faintly we hear some chatter. Then the six of them must be gathered in the main room where the microphone is, for suddenly we can hear clearly.

"I called the meeting to let you all know the *Malchik* is on his way," Becca says.

There's a general murmur of approval and relief that things are going to happen. Someone claps his hands.

Tom and I look at each other. We've just learned the bomb is coming — a devastating piece of news — and we've learned who's in charge. I've suspected all along that Becca's the general and the guys are louies. Is it hard for them as Muslims to have a woman in charge? Something else I might exploit if I get the chance.

"I don't yet know exactly when it will arrive," she goes on. "The ship has left Rotterdam. It goes next to the container port in Elizabeth. It should take about five days to cross the Atlantic, assuming the weather's favorable. We have less than a week to get ready."

There's another general murmur. I look at Tom, but he doesn't say anything. I'm surprised they still have to "get ready." I'd have thought it would all be planned in detail. Maybe it's a strategy to wait for something definite.

"Yusef and Hussein, you'll need to go now to a rest area — the one called Vince Lombardi is closest; many container trucks stop there on their way to the port. When you see one parked there, one that has no cargo, wait until the driver returns to it. Kill him and dump the body where it won't be seen. Here's the manifest for the cargo you're picking up. Put it in the glove compartment and destroy any manifest that's there."

There's a pause, and we hear papers rustling.

"You can see the manifest describes the cargo and authorizes the unloading."

There's silence for a few minutes.

"I want each of you to go over your job, and we can figure out the details and iron out any problems," she says. "Al, you start."

"OK." I recognize Al's voice from our brief telephone conversation. "Originally, I was supposed to make sure the power is off in the whole city as the truck comes in. There are several ways to do it. The city is connected to the northeast grid system, and any simple outage will just cause the city to pull in power from the surrounding area. So we can't just blow up a transformer. We have to blow up a couple of substations. I can set that up in a few hours. But there's a problem. If they think an attack is under way, they'll close the bridges and tunnels, and we won't be able get the truck in. This means we have to make it look like a natural blackout so they won't close the bridges and tunnels. We need to make sure the truck can get in."

"Would it be better to get the truck in first, and then pull the plug?" Becca asked.

"Well, that's what I think. Then it'd be easier to get the power off. We have to either turn the power off in a way that convinces them it's not a terrorist attack, or get the truck in first."

"Originally, as I recall from our meeting in Peshawar," another voice speaks, and Tom and I look at each other. There's no accent. Probably it's Nat. "We thought the confusion of a general outage would make it easier to get the truck in, but now that we know the policy is to shut down the tunnels and bridges, I think we should get the truck in first then turn the power off." This is Nat speaking, I'm now sure.

Another voice speaks, and I can hear the Arabic accent. "But what about us? How do we get out if the bridges and tunnels are closed?" I can't tell who it is, not Al's roomie Muhammad. More likely one of the brothers. I look at Tom and mouth the word "driver."

The voice goes on. "We're not 14-year-old zealots who think we're going to martyr ourselves into paradise."

"You can leave by boat," says Becca. "We have lots of money, and I'm going to buy two fast boats, one on each river. I'll be in one on the Hudson, Nat in one on the East River. In a fast boat, you can get far away in an hour. Which boat you take will depend on where you park the truck."

Tom and I look at each other again, and we both mouth the words "one hour."

"I am not so sure," replies a deeper voice, also with an Arabic accent. "We can get down the river and out into the harbor, possibly past Staten Island, but not much farther. Could we not have more time?"

"The longer the truck sits parked, the more likely someone will become suspicious."

"And are we still going to park it in Times Square?"

"I don't like that," says Becca. "I never have. It's such a crowded area. The truck'll become suspicious immediately, or worse they'll tow it away outside the city. Remember the guy whose bomb didn't go off?"

"Well where should we park it?"

"The beauty of the *Malchik* is there'll be complete destruction within a mile and a half radius. It doesn't matter where we park it. The city's going to be heavily damaged." There's triumph in Becca's voice, and I marvel at the hatred. Horrible as her life has been, it doesn't seem like an explanation. There must be something else.

"Then why not park it in Hoboken so we don't have to risk an inspection by crossing a bridge or tunnel?" one of the drivers asks. I still don't know which is which.

"That's Plan C," says Becca. "That's what we'll do if all the bridges and tunnels have been closed. But there's also the possibility they'll close the bridges and tunnels to Manhattan but leave the Verrazano Narrows Bridge to Brooklyn open. In that case we follow Plan B, which is that you'll take the truck into Brooklyn and leave it as close to the base of the Brooklyn Bridge as possible. It will then also be very close to Wall St., which is our main target."

Tom and I look at each other again.

"And if the Verrazano Narrows Bridge is also closed?" asks the deeper of the two Arabic-sounding voices.

"Then you follow Plan C, as I said, and park it in Hoboken," comes the answer quickly. I notice she doesn't react to the driver's slowness in understanding the plans.

"OK," says the first Arabic-tinged voice. "From Hoboken or

from Brooklyn, we can steal a car and get away. But suppose the bridges and tunnels are all open, and we drive into Manhattan. We still have not settled the question of where to park the truck."

"I know," says Becca. "That's Plan A, our first choice. The truck has to be close to one of the rivers because they'll quickly close the bridges and tunnels if they find the truck or become suspicious in any way, and you'll need to get to one of the boats. After he's turned off the power, Al will go to one of the two boats, whichever is closer. Muhammad also will go to a boat, but we haven't discussed his role. We'll do that now."

"In a terrorist attack, the City pulls the trains into the nearest station." It's Muhammad speaking. "Then the people get out and stay in the station underground if they suspect a bomb or come up into the air if they expect a gas attack. For us it won't matter. They'll all die anyway." I can't help shuddering when I hear him say that, and Tom, bless his heart, reaches over and holds my hand.

"What'll you do?" This is Becca speaking with authority again.

"I can arrange to stop the trains before they pull into the stations. People will have to get out and find their way to a station in the dark. There will be much panic."

"But won't they survive the blast if they're deep in the tunnel?" It's Nat's voice.

"Yes. So I thought it best to do nothing. Their policy of discharging passengers in the stations will cause more death than anything else."

"I think that's a wise decision," says Becca. "We won't stop the trains."

"We still don't know where to park." One of the drivers again.

"I know," Becca says. "Plan A is for you to bring the truck in over the George Washington Bridge. It's farther from the ship, I know, but it's much simpler to get to. I think we shouldn't go through the tunnels. The police guard the tunnels more closely, and they're more likely to stop us."

"Yes, that's right," says Muhammad. "There are random stops at the tunnels, but not the bridges, and someone watches the tunnel entrances at all times, so if they find out about us and can identify the truck, they could stop us. The bridges aren't even watched."

"So," Becca goes on. "You'll listen to the radio as you drive up the New Jersey Turnpike. They'll announce and broadcast all closures. If all bridges are closed, including the Verrazano Narrows Bridge, we'll use Plan C. You'll drive to Hoboken, park as near to the river as possible, set the device for one hour, steal a car, and drive to Chicago. You know where to go in Chicago." She says it as if she's sure they know, and although there's no answer, Tom and I imagine them nodding their heads.

"If the bridges and tunnels to Manhattan are closed, but the Verrazano Narrows Bridge is open, then we'll use Plan B. You'll drive into Brooklyn and park by the Brooklyn Bridge. We'll be in touch by cell phone, and Nat or I will pick you up in one of the boats. Or you can steal a car and drive to Chicago. If you can't get back across the river, the end of Long Island will be safe."

"But where will we park if we're in Manhattan?" The voice sounds exasperated.

"I'm going to look into it. Nat and I will investigate various locations. After you come over the George Washington Bridge — Plan A — you could park right there, and there would still be major destruction, but not Wall St. Still, the psychological effect will be much stronger if the bomb goes off in the middle of Manhattan, so Nat and I will try to find a good place, and we'll plan a route for you. We'll meet again as soon as Nat and I have finished our investigations. Meanwhile go back to your jobs. Act normal. But think about potential problems."

"The plan for getting the container off the ship is still the same?" asks one of the drivers.

"Yes, it's still the same." Tom and I both squeeze our hands at the same time. We have so much information, but it'd be nice to know when and where they'll get the container off the ship. Then we could stop them earlier, before they even get close to New York.

Al speaks up again. "I think we should not turn the city power off."

"Give your reasons," says Becca.

"When the bomb goes off, there'll be total confusion anyway. Turning the power off won't add much. And if we turn it off before, they'll know something's going to happen, or they'll assume that it is."

"These are good arguments." There is silence. My guess is she's looking around at the group to see what their reaction is, but no one says anything.

"I agree with you," she says finally. "We won't turn the power off."

"In this case," says Al, "Muhammad and I have no further tasks to perform."

"That's right," says Becca. "You might as well go home." I think she must mean back to whatever country they came from. It's the only interpretation that makes sense.

The meeting is over. We can hear people saying "goodbye" and "see you later" and "*insha'Allah*." We hear the door open and close several times, and then it's quiet again.

***

We look at each other.

"They sound like amateurs," Tom says. "I can see why the bureau hasn't taken them seriously."

"They may be amateurs, but they could still carry out their plot."

"Right." Tom is thinking.

I have a strange mixture of feelings. I'm scared, of course, but two other feelings, both powerful, lay over the fear like heavy tarpaulins. One is a determination to stop them — a fierce, mother-tiger feeling. This is my city, my home, and my friends, and I live here. I'll do anything to protect it. The other is a surprising urge to make sure nothing is left undone in my life, that loose ends get tied up. Tom's face looks as though he too is feeling a mixture, but he stands, as though ready to leave.

"I have to tell the director," he says. And I stand up too.

"Don't you have to tell someone in Homeland Security?"

"I'm supposed to, or really the director is supposed to."

"There's a 'but' hanging in the air, and it sure as hell isn't yours." I pat his flat little behind and feel very racy and bold as I do it. It's a good feeling. It has something to do with tying up loose ends.

He laughs. "The 'but' that's hanging has to do with Homeland Security."

"Still?" I wrinkle up my face with the question.

"Those guys at Homeland Security…" He breaks off the sentence.

"What about them?"

"Not many people know this, but those guys at Homeland Security don't know what they're doing."

Most journalists do know about this problem, but I want to hear how he's going to explain it to me. It was shocking to me when I first heard it, and I'm not a person who shocks easily. I want to hear Tom explain it from his point of view. "What's the matter with them?"

"When they created the office, the president appointed his buddies to the leadership positions. I think half of his college class was working in government then. But Homeland Security was a new agency, and there were many management positions to fill. They were all filled with the president's friends, or with the friends of friends. But none of them had any experience or ability in law enforcement. And that pattern established a culture in the agency that's still influential."

My reporter's ears are back on. We've all heard about cronyism, and plenty of stories have been written about it, but I don't think we knew it had extended into Homeland Security, at least not down to the levels where it would influence operations.

"I'm surprised it's affected day-to-day operations."

"New leadership is always the crucial part of any agency. If the leadership is rotten, the good people all leave. No one wants to work for an incompetent boss. It's a horrible experience. Even the bosses don't like it. Imagine having the people under you know the answers to problems you can't figure out. So the agency gradually becomes less and less competent because the good people leave and the incompetent people stay."

"Why is it the good ones who leave?"

"First, because they're the ones who feel the talent inversion the most."

I make a mental note of the phrase "talent inversion." I've never heard anyone use it before. Talent at the bottom, incompetence at the top, like a cold front over a warm front. Guaranteed instability in government as in the weather. "And second?"

"Because they can. The people who have talent and experience are always the most mobile. People want to hire them. So they leave for jobs where there are people with talent and good leadership. Today that means they leave government."

"So this means you're thinking about not telling the Homeland Security people we know there's a terrorist cell planning to set off an atomic bomb in New York City?" My eyebrows are so high, they may be hidden behind my curly blonde bangs. And my bangs are short.

"Fortunately, it's not my call."

"The director's?" I suggest.

"Sure. I have to tell him. And he's a good guy — competent, sure of himself, bright — but I'm going to suggest he keep the investigation in our office because if we turn it over there's a good chance it'll get botched, and we can't afford to have that happen."

"You and he may get in trouble," I offer a little apologetically because I know it isn't a constructive comment.

"That really doesn't matter. If we succeed in stopping them, we'll be forgiven. If we fail…" His voice drifts off, and I realize if they fail, none of us will be around to worry about who's stepped on whose toes.

"We already have great surveillance right here." He jabs his index finger down toward the floor of my apartment. "We're gonna know what they're doing before they do it. You'll see a lot of me in the next week or two." He smiles as he says this, and I recognize a melting feeling. My old friend. Sex is never far away, I think, no matter what the circumstances. My knees even feel a little weak. I think again about tying up loose ends, and I realize for the first time Tom is a loose end. We've been seeing each other for a couple of years, sleeping together when we can, but there's been no actual commitment. Now it may be too late.

"That's OK." I can hear the huskiness in my voice, completely giving me away. He takes my face in his hands and kisses me then, and he keeps kissing me, and he puts his arms around me, and I just hang onto him and let myself go like I'm being washed out to sea in a warm tide and don't care where the current's taking me. I might as well be 14 again for all the control I have over myself. I feel his tongue caressing my lips then parting them and exploring my mouth. His hands move over my back and down to my butt. He pulls me in tight, and I can feel him, hard and eager. I'm completely ready. I'm just about to start undoing buttons when his arms suddenly slacken.

"We have a lot to do." He breaks away.

"Yes." But I'd have said "yes" no matter what he suggested.

He gives me a look that's tender but resigned to the fact that there's too much to do to be fooling around, no matter how nice it is.

"We'll take this up later," he says. "I promise."

"OK. I'm going to hold you to it." I could have worked in one of my little jokes on that sentence, but for the first time in a long time, I don't want to. I'm not feeling flirtatious anymore. It's gone way past that.

Then, quickly, he's all business, the same old Tom.

"I have to get to the office and talk to the director."

"I have to talk to Colonel Haldane." The huskiness has almost left my voice.

"Why?"

"She's someone in government I trust. She's got good ideas. And I guess she's become a friend." The last idea surprises me. It's been a long time since I had a friend who wasn't a man, and I like the idea.

"OK. But try to keep her from going to Homeland Security, at least for the time being."

"I think she has the same opinion about them you do."

"Good." And he walks out the door.

I go back to my recording devices and listen, but there's no sound. It doesn't seem likely they're asleep already. I figure they must be reading or working on the computer. I make a mental note to check the computer report in the morning. Then I get myself ready for bed. I don't feel much like sleeping, but there's going to be so much going on tomorrow and for the next few days that I know I'll need the rest. So I get into bed and lie there, thinking mostly about Tom, but occasionally about the destruction of New York City.

20. THE TRAP

Thursday, 7 a.m. New York City

I slept poorly, and I'm still scuffling around in my slippers at 7:00 in the morning when the phone rings. Some people can't wait for every house to have a videophone. I can wait. Most of the time when I'm home, I'm not a pretty sight.

It's Col. Haldane, and she comes right to the point.

"Not too long ago you told me there was a mole in our department."

"I remember."

"Can you help us catch him?"

"I'll do anything I can."

"I know you're listening in on a terrorist group. I want to send three different specific pieces of misinformation to the terrorist leaders via three different people, one of whom I'm sure is the mole. When you hear the information coming back to the cell that you're monitoring, we'll know who the mole is. D'you understand?"

"Sure."

"Can you tell me what you know? I'll keep it to myself."

"OK. I will. I think it might be a good idea to let you in on it anyway. You might be able to help."

"I'm glad you feel that way."

"But is it safe to talk about this over the phone? Someone might be listening."

"It's OK. I'm not in my office. So what's up in Manhattan?"

"There's no way to play it down. These people are planning to set off an atomic bomb of the Little Boy type right here in

Manhattan. We know quite a lot, but not everything, about their plan."

"D'you know when this is going to happen?" It amazes me she can hear this news and keep her cool. I wonder if she's been expecting it.

"No, and they don't either, but we will soon. The container ship is en route from Rotterdam."

"D'you know the name of the ship?"

"No, I'm afraid we don't, but we're working on it."

"OK. What's the terrorists' plan?"

"Well, there are actually three plans, contingencies for different conditions. But in any case, two guys are going to drive the container off the ship in New Jersey, come up the New Jersey Turnpike, and if no one has suspected anything and the bridges and tunnels are open, they'll come into Manhattan over the George Washington Bridge, drive to some location in the center of Manhattan — it hasn't been decided where yet — park the truck, set a timing device for one hour, and leave."

"It's not a suicide operation then?"

"No, they don't want it to be, certainly not the drivers."

"How are they going to escape? They have to get pretty far away."

"They're going to have two fast boats waiting, one on the Hudson, one on the East River. They'll go to whichever one is closest to where they end up parking the truck."

"Jesus! It's planned out, isn't it?"

"Except for a few details, yes."

"What will they do if the bridges and tunnels are closed?"

"Then they'll park the truck in Hoboken." There's a little silence. She's probably taking notes. "But if the Verrazano Narrows Bridge is open, they'll park the truck in Brooklyn at the foot of the Brooklyn Bridge."

"So there are three plans, with the truck going to a different place for each one."

"That's right."

"Thanks, Kimmie. Let me work out some disinformation to send out, and I'll get back to you."

We hang up.

I start to straighten up the place. God knows it needs it. But I don't get very far. In 20 minutes she calls back.

"Here's what I'm going to do. I'm going to tell each of the three guys a different story. The one who's the mole is going to send it back to the leaders who will tell the New York cell. The first story is there's a new device for monitoring the cargo of a truck as it passes under an overpass, but the device can't penetrate a certain kind of paint that they put on ships — copper bottom paint. Al Qaeda will want the drivers to paint their cowling, you know that big thing that sticks up above the cab, with this paint so the nature of the cargo will stay secret. The second story is the coast guard is equipping its boats with a device like the reconnaissance planes use, a laser that can be beamed at a boat, the direction and range then radioed to a satellite and coordinated with a GPS on the coast guard boat, so a plane or helicopter can pinpoint a boat in the water. But painting the boat flat black, like a stealth bomber, can foil it. It's a little far-fetched, but I'm counting on these guys not being very sophisticated."

"I got it."

"The third story is there's a mole in the cell itself. I'm not sure how they'll react to that, but I'm hoping the cell leader will talk to one of the other cell members, one that can be trusted, and you'll overhear the conversation."

"OK. I got the three stories. Are you going to do this right away?"

"You bet. Today." I like her decisiveness.

"OK, I'll be listening."

"I'm counting on you." The way she says it makes me want to be worthy of her confidence.

"And I'm counting on you for anything that'll help stop these guys."

"Let me think about it for a while and get back to you. My first thought is it would be best to identify the container ship and keep it out at sea so there's never any danger to the city."

"I haven't heard anything that would help identify the ship. Could we keep all container ships away from Elizabeth?"

"I don't think so, but it's a thought. If we knew the timing better, within a day or so, we might be able to close the port, but that's something your FBI friend will have to ask the governor of New Jersey."

"I'll try to find out more about it."

We hang up.

I realize I've taken on another job, and I already have more jobs than any person should have. Also there's Tom, and I want to leave room in my life for him. I still have to write stories, or at least make my boss believe I'm writing them. Well that won't be hard.

***

I get myself ready for work. I'm in such a hurry, I catch myself wishing the shower water would run faster, and I leave without breakfast. I hate to skip breakfast. At the office, pastries and other good stuff are always available. I call them "conspiratorial pastries" because if we become fat and unattractive we'll all just sit at our computers and work. These pastries roll by seductively on a little cart all day long, which I try to stay away from, and I would have, even this morning, honest, but the conversation with Colonel Haldane is a perfect excuse to indulge, so I compromise, if that's the word, and stop at a little deli a block away from the office and order a regular coffee to go and a kind of Danish I like. This way I'm not patronizing the conspiratorial company pastry cart.

Back on the sidewalk, I struggle to get the plastic top off my coffee without dropping my pastry so I can have a few sips before I need my extra hand to open the door. The plastic top pops off suddenly, and I stop quickly and hold the cup away from my body to make sure I don't spill coffee on my coat. As I jerk to a stop with my coffee cup out in front of me like a blind man's white cane, I hear a sharp 'pffft' kind of sound. My coffee cup explodes in my hand, and I drop what's left of it. A hole appears in the store window next to me.

It takes a second before I realize someone's shooting at me, and I jump into the store entrance.

From the doorway I peek around the side. A car's speeding away into the downtown traffic. I can't be sure if it's the car the shot came from, and I don't get the license number anyway. I was too busy running and hiding. I look around. There's no one near me. I take out my cell phone and try to dial 911, but my hands are shaking, and it takes several tries before I can tell the person that someone's taken a shot at me. The cops come quickly. The city may be dangerous, but the protection is very reassuring.

A young officer gets out of the car from the passenger side and walks in my direction. I leave my ineffective hiding place and walk toward him. A female officer was driving, and she's still sitting in the driver's seat as the other officer and I meet in the sidewalk. I wonder about pairing up male and female officers. Doesn't it lead to sexual attraction, affairs, then probably recriminations, domestic issues, divorce? It seems dangerous.

What's wrong with my mind that it wanders into these mental alleyways even though someone's just tried to kill me? Isn't my self-preservation at all important?

"Someone took a shot at me. Look at the window." I point at the little hole and the spider web of cracks around it." And that's what's left of my coffee." I kick the mangled cup with my toe.

"OK." The cop seems a little unconcerned. He inspects the hole in the window. "No one else seems to have noticed." He looks around. He's right. People seem mildly curious but no more. It's the New York police-incident look. If there were a dead body on the street, some people would have stopped, but not many. Everyone has some place they need to be. I do too, and I hope this won't take too long.

"I think it had a silencer on it," I tell the cop, trying to keep my voice from shaking. "I don't know much about guns, but it made a kind of 'pffft' sound, not a bang."

"Hmmm. That's what a shot from a silenced gun sounds like." He seems to be convinced that at least I didn't make up the whole story. "Why would anyone want to shoot at you?"

"I'm a reporter." I dig my ID out of my purse and show it to him. "Sometimes I write stories people don't like." He pulls back only a little because he's too young to have lost his close-up vision, and he looks at the ID carefully, reading my name.

"Did you write something like that recently, Ms. Hansen?" In New York, the policemen are careful to be politically correct. I'll bet it's different in Dubuque.

"Yes, as a matter of fact I did." I tell him people have told me to "be careful." Behind him his partner's getting out of the car, looking around, and walking slowly toward us.

"Could this be those people? The ones you wrote about?"

"It could. People warned me there might be retaliation."

"And who are they?"

"I was afraid you might ask that. The story I wrote described men working in the procurement office of the armed services who demoted a whistleblower there — a Colonel Haldane."

"Oh, yeah, I read that story. You wrote that?" He moves a little closer to me, suddenly more interested. I guess I'm a little famous, at least here in the city. "Wasn't the vice president's office involved somehow?"

"Yes, I did, and they were — definitely." His partner has joined us. She's young, very pretty in a petite way, though oddly bulky in the torso, but she looks ready to take care of herself. She doesn't say anything but keeps looking around. Apparently she's the security detail. Her job's to make sure the big black car doesn't run around the block and come back for a second shot. I'm grateful.

"Nice work. But watch out. Those guys are heavy hitters. You do need to be careful."

"I wish people would stop telling me that. I don't know what I can do to be more careful." There's a little desperation in my voice, I guess, because he takes the statement seriously.

"You could wear a vest. We all do now, almost all the time." He pulls his shirt open, just a little between two buttons, to show me that underneath he's wearing something thick and black. He taps on his chest with his fingertip, and it makes a clacking sound.

"I'll think about it." I wonder what a bulletproof vest would do for my figure. I can see he looks chesty and bulky. Then I look at his partner. The bulky torso lady. From her face and her hips, I see she's very slender. I wonder whether it's worth sacrificing what sex appeal I have left for better security.

"At least when you're out in the street." He counters my hesitation.

"OK. I can see the value in that." He must think I'm a nut. I want to ask his partner some questions — does the hard surface irritate her nipples? Maybe she protects them by wearing something soft inside her bra? A camisole might do the trick too. Things I'm pretty sure the guy wouldn't know.

He scribbles something on a piece of paper.

"Here's a place where you can get one." He hands it to me. "I've also written the department's internal number on there. You can call them to see what they've found out."

"Thanks." I put it in my purse without looking at it. I want to get off the street, even though New York's finest are right there with me. I don't think the vice president's goons would care much about a police presence.

The female cop nods her head. The male finishes writing something and asks me to sign it. Then we say our goodbyes.

I hurry to the *Times* building and go to my workstation with a certain gratitude. But I discover I dropped my bag of pastries in the street along with my exploded coffee cup. I'll have to go to the company cart after all.

There's nothing boring about commuting.

***

At my desk, I can't concentrate. I open my purse and look at the paper the cop gave me. I call the NYPD special number and ask what they might have found out. They've examined the scene already and retrieved the slug. That's progress, I think. Then I look at the address the cop gave me for a place to get a bulletproof vest. It's just around the corner, and I can't think straight enough to work anyway, so I go to the store to see what's fashionable in torso bulkers.

I try on a bulletproof vest like the cop suggested, pulling it tight over my dress, then I put on my overcoat, which is a cream-colored velour kind of material — very soft and cuddly — but with the flak jacket underneath it I look like a slightly dirty snowball.

Wearing the vest not only makes me look funny, but it also makes me think about the parts of my body that aren't covered but which I'd just as soon not be shot in, starting with my head. Of course if I were shot in the head, I'd probably be dead, so it wouldn't matter. That is, however, no consolation whatsoever. I don't want to be dead. That's the point. Also I can't help thinking how terrible my hair would look with blood in it, or how badly an exit wound would mess up my face. I think about my arms and legs too, which could be broken and scarred by bullets. I like them the way they are, thank you. And my pelvic area. Considering my relationship with Tom, that particular part of me seems much more important, even foremost, and I want to keep it intact for both of us. I wonder if that thought has occurred to him. I take the thing off, shake my head at the store clerk, and head for the door. I stop and look through the window at the traffic going by and the scurrying pedestrians. It seems like a good idea to take the day off.

I call Tom and ask him to drive me home. I feel like I'm being really nervy; he's so busy, but he's properly solicitous. "Find out where the back entrance is," he says first. And when I do, I hear, "I can get there in 20 minutes." Then he hangs up.

Sure enough, when I finally poke my head out the back door, I spot Tom's car at the end of the alley and run to it. In the car, Tom gives me a long, worried, glad-that-you're-alive look that warms me inside the way a shot of Wild Turkey used to.

"I called the NYPD," I tell him once we're headed uptown.

"What'd you find?"

"Only that the slug came from a Glock something or other," I answer. "The crime investigation unit dug it out of a mannequin's kneecap in the shop window. It was pretty mangled up from going through the plate glass, but you know how good those guys are."

He nods. "That's the kind of gun a professional hit man would use."

"Well, you didn't think the vice president himself was going to come after me, did you?" I answer sharply.

"No," he says in a hoarse voice. "I didn't."

I'm scared for my life, and he's thinking about catching a crook, doing his job. "Don't you know how close I came to getting killed?" I scream at him. Then I look at him driving. He's tough, masculine. "Sorry for being so short," I say after an introspective moment. I seem to be having a lot of those lately. We're quiet on the rest of the drive uptown, until we turn the corner onto 81st Street.

"There's the flowerpot." I point up at it through the windshield. "They're going to meet." I look at my watch. "Probably in about an hour," figuring it would be the same as last time. "Come on up. We'll listen."

"Sure," he says, and I feel my heart start to pound. There's a funny feeling in my legs too, like they're looser, and I have to focus on walking.

We take the elevator up to my apartment. As we step out and its doors close behind us, I take the key out of my purse and start toward my door.

"Wait a second," Tom says, grabbing my shoulder from behind. I think he's going to spin me around and kiss me impulsively in the hallway, and I have my mouth open a little, just getting ready.

"Let me," he says, taking the key from me.

"Sure," I say, and hand it to him. Impulsive kisses are not Tom's style.

He puts the key in the lock and waits a second then turns it and waits another second, listening. Then he turns the knob, again slowly. I realize he's doing everything step by step, testing to make sure there's no bomb wired to detonate when something moves. And then we're inside. No boom, no bomb.

I make some coffee, and we turn on the speakers so we can hear what's going on in the apartment, but there are no voices. They're in there — the occasional sound of footsteps and dishes rattling — but they're not talking. Why don't they ever talk to each other, ask how the other's day was, did you hear anything about the bomb, just chit-chat, the kind of small talk terrorists around the world make at the end of a workday? But there's nothing. I start to think about dinner.

***

"I can make you an omelet." I offer food while Tom is still taking off his overcoat and setting a chair up by the window so he can watch the street.

"Omelet's fine, thanks." He almost shrugs.

"We could send out for Chinese or pizza, if you want. You haven't ever tasted my cooking," I add.

"I'll take my chances." The lopsided grin.

I go into the kitchen while he stays with the listening devices in case something comes in. I put on a little apron, break six eggs, cut up some peppers, wipe off and chop up some mushrooms, grate a lot of cheese, mix everything together, and throw in a pinch of thyme and remix it. I wonder if I should put in another pinch of thyme, and I realize I know little about Tom's general likes and dislikes. I come out of the kitchen.

"Do you like hot sauce on your eggs?" I have my fingers crossed behind my back.

"No, not particularly."

187

I smile and uncross my fingers. "You've just won the contest as the best guy in New York."

"Just because I don't like hot sauce?" He's wrinkled up his eyebrows in some strange but cute, asymmetrical way.

"Well, yeah."

"OK." The brow wrinkles smooth out into a big grin. "But it's a funny contest."

"Just be glad you won. Don't fight with the judge."

I go back into the kitchen, chuckling, put an omelet pan onto a burner and pour the eggs into it. I wiggle my hips in a little dance as I stand in front of the stove. I tilt the pan and pull the cooked eggs up a little, letting the runny part drain down into the hot bottom of the pan, just like they do on the TV cooking shows. I haven't been watching them since I got promoted, but when I was writing the obits, I'd watched them every night while I waited for the pizza guy to come. I always enjoyed the irony of watching cooking shows while waiting for pizza. Like having your cake and eating… no that's a little too much metaphor. I cut up some fresh tomatoes and drizzle a little olive oil on them, followed by a pinch of salt. My dad used to do that, and it still makes me think of him to fix fresh tomatoes like that. He wasn't much of a cook either; he would have liked Tom, I think with a little sigh.

I fold the omelet over then peek out the door. Tom has given up on the listening devices and is looking out the window, and I know he's watching for the other guys to come home and see the signal. I bring out two plates.

"You want to hold this on your lap so you can watch, or come to the table?" I stop, holding the two plates, waiting for the answer.

"Table." He gets up. He's not overly talkative.

"Would you like something to drink with it?" I put the

plates down. "Water, juice, coffee, soda?" My fingers start to cross again. I'm almost praying he doesn't ask for beer. It would have killed the whole romance thing.

"Coffee sounds good."

My fingers relax, and I grin again. It's the famous sitting-in-the-catbird-seat, shit-eating grin of the person who keeps hearing good news that could have been bad news. I drank a lot when I was younger. For a reporter in New York, drinking is basic. I'd say alcohol is one of the four basic food groups for reporters, but it's an old, stale joke, and besides, alcohol to a reporter is more basic than that. Of course I found out later the whole alcohol-is-basic-to-reporting idea is a crock. The best reporters work sober.

Four years ago I woke up one Sunday morning and went to the computer to finish a story that was due in an hour. I was nursing a headache and a disgusting cup of coffee at the same time, swallowed four aspirins, went to the bathroom and threw up then watched my fingers trembling on the keys. That was the end of drinking for me. Who needs that when you can just as easily catch pneumonia and get the same feeling? I went to AA for a while, and that was a big help because it wasn't as easy to stop as I thought it would be. I still go sometimes, but not that often, and now it's the gratitude for being sober that sends me there rather than the fear I might start drinking again. After I stopped drinking, I discovered how disgusting someone smells after they've had a few, and that's why my fingers relaxed. I wouldn't have been able to kiss Tom with beer on his breath.

I pour two coffees and sit down. I forget to take my apron off, but I don't think he notices. He's watching the way my hips move as I walk to the table, trying not to spill the overfilled mugs. I try to make them move just a little more suggestively, but in the attempt I almost spill the coffee, so I give up. But I like the feeling of his eyes on me. I put the mugs down slowly and sit down with him.

"If we're lucky, we might hear where they're going to park the truck."

"For sure." He forks a load of omelet into his mouth and swallows quickly. "And finding out when the cargo is going to arrive would be even better. Hey, this is really good!" I smile. Both at him and to myself. I want to take all my clothes off, but I just know this is the wrong time. Instead, I keep the conversation businesslike.

"When a container comes in on one of these RoRo ships, the owners must be informed. Does that information get published?"

"I'm not sure." He shovels in another load of omelet. He eats fast and carelessly. He might as well be filling his gas tank. I shouldn't have worried about putting in too much thyme.

"It's probably in the shipping news." Ever the reporter, I know many sources of information. "If you know what ship your container is on, you just watch for the docking date. They probably have drivers at the dock who take off the cargoes nobody claims right away too."

"Mmmhmm." He seems to agree. "We don't know the ship though, do we?"

"No, but we might find that out tonight. And we ought to be able to narrow it down. How many container ships could there be sailing from Rotterdam to Elizabeth?"

He shrugs. "Maybe quite a few. But narrowing it down is a first step."

"Colonel Haldane said she thought the governor might be able to close the port if we could narrow the date down."

"Yes, that's a possibility. But I'm not sure how quick the governor will be able to cut off such a big source of revenue. I haven't ever had anything quite like this come up before."

"Welcome to the club."

***

After we've eaten the omelet and a little ice cream I find in the freezer, we go into the living room and sit on the couch. The speakers are on, the guys have arrived, and the meeting is underway, but it sounds as though we didn't miss much. Becca's going through a list of questions she has. She's asking if they've gotten weapons. Apparently they want to be well armed, even though their plan is based on secrecy. I don't quite understand that, but then I'm not a terrorist. Every one of them has found some kind of gun, and they're laughing about how easy it was.

"Criminals are treated very kindly in this country," one of them says.

Tom's taking notes. He wants to know exactly what kind of arms they have. He dots an i, or maybe it's a period, but he does it with a flourish, and I can tell he has all the information he needs about their weaponry.

"It's all being recorded, you know." I remind him it isn't necessary to take notes.

"I just like to make sure I have it," he answers. I shrug. If he wants to take notes, it's OK with me.

Over the speakers, Becca's talking. "Nat and I have found a good place for you to park the truck."

There's a little murmur, which ends abruptly, as though Becca raised her hand to shush them.

"It's under the West Side Highway, around 79th St., not far from here. And real close to the marina."

"I know the area. It sounds good — there's lots of room. But it isn't close to Wall St." It's Yusef or Hussein.

"I know," Becca says, "but Nat and I don't think it'll matter.

There'll be terrible destruction into the heart of the city. Wall St. will be damaged too. We have to balance the exact target against the psychological impact of getting the bomb into the city. The 79th St. location will be easy to get to, so there'll be less likelihood of getting stopped."

There's a long silence, during which somebody could object, but no one does.

"And the route?" I can't tell if it's Yusef or Hussein. I've never really learned to tell them apart.

"Remember this is only Plan A, if the bridges and tunnels are open."

Someone says "yes," and I hear "*insha'Allah*."

"You come over the George Washington Bridge. Use the upper level. It's easier to get to the local streets from it. You'll see a sign for Broadway. Take that exit and you'll be on a side street that meets up with Broadway. Turn right and you'll be heading south on Broadway. Stay on it until you get into the 70s then take the first westbound street and go to the end. You'll see the overhead roadway. You can park the truck under it. There should be lots of spaces. I'll be at the pier at 79th St. Get a car tomorrow and drive the route a couple of times to get used to it. We only have a day."

Tom and I look at each other, a little puzzled.

"Did we miss something?" I whisper.

He shrugs his shoulders, not wanting to risk missing something more.

"We've bought the boats and docked them. Nat's is off 23rd St. on the East River. We're all armed. The three plans are in place. You're going to buy the antifouling paint and paint the truck cowling. We're all set. In a day we'll be a part of history."

Hearing that, I understand at least one part of her motive. She wants fame, even if it is in fact infamy. I remember what I read in her dossier, and try to figure out how a need for fame or recognition would fit into it. But I can't come up with a plausible theory. But when the time comes to write all this up, I think, I'll have the basis of an excellent psychological portrait, even if there are some loose ends. I can see the headline "Portrait of a Terrorist" on the page with my by-line. I guess I want recognition too. Well what's the difference between us, I wonder. What makes Becca willing to go to extremes, while I worry about having a second bagel for breakfast.

We hear the door open and shut several times. Then Nat says, "I'll probably not see you again."

Of course, they have the cell phones. And I'll be able to hear when they use them.

"Wait a minute!" I yell, grabbing Tom's arm by the sleeve of his coat. "They said something about painting the truck cowling, didn't they?" I'm asking him for confirmation. "I have to tell Colonel Haldane. That tells her who the mole is."

That's when I realize we missed the first part of the meeting. "They must have started the meeting while we were eating. They discussed the truck cowling then."

"And they know when the ship's coming in. We have to know that. Play it back."

I go to the recorder and rewind it. When I put it on play, it's the previous meeting. I fast-forward. There's the sound of someone singing opera. It must be one of the neighbors. I keep pushing the fast-forward button, but every time I stop, all I hear is the neighbor's bel canto, and then I hear the recording end.

"It ran out." Slowly the awful consequences dawn on me.

Tom looks grim. "You mean we didn't record the first part of the meeting?" It's not really a question — more of a death sentence.

"Oh, shit, no." I shake my head in disbelief. "The neighbor

was singing, and that triggered the voice activation, so it kept recording. Then it ran out of room before the meeting started." It's so frustrating I could cry.

"So we don't know when the ship's coming in." He says this nodding slowly. It's devastating news, and he's working hard to accept it. We've been counting on knowing everything they know, but now we're missing the most crucial piece of information. And the way they said goodbye sounded as though this was the last meeting. Of course maybe Nat and Becca will start talking to each other, and then we might hear more, but I'm not optimistic about it.

"What can we do?" I feel helpless — not a way I feel very often.

"I have to talk to my boss and see if we can't get the governor to close the port for a few days." He looks worried.

"And can you?"

"I don't know. Without specifics, I doubt a judge will approve. But we've got to try."

He turns then and grabs me in his arms and kisses me. It's almost ferocious, as if he were some wild creature in the forest. At first I think he might be angry with me; it's so sudden and rough. I hang onto him. He isn't angry at all. But now we may really die. I feel his desperation — the muscles around his neck and shoulders feel hard — and I feel desperate myself. The future's bleak. I'd started to dream a little, and now I can't. It's cut off. No dreaming allowed. I hold him even tighter.

Ferocity and desperation turn into lust. We tear our clothes off. Buttons fly, zippers grate, even while we're kissing. I throw my bra down. Deep, guttural moaning sounds. I'm not sure if they're from him or me. Our clothes fall in a heap, and we're holding each other, naked. My bare breasts are crushed against his chest. I can feel his erection pressing against me, and I feel myself getting wet. He grabs my hand and pulls me into the bedroom, where we fall on the bed.

It isn't soft and tender. It isn't romantic. It's savage and eager, desperately urgent. I come the moment he enters me, and I can feel my spasms squeezing him. In a moment his movements speed up, and then it's over, and we roll apart.

Jesus! What was that? I wonder. I've never felt anything like it. Lust brought on by the thought of imminent death? Can it work that way? I guess it can. He looks at me then with a tenderness I've never seen in a man's eyes before.

He mumbles some words of apology and gets up. I'm only a little slower. We both have to get busy. What were we thinking? I ask myself. But I know the answer. We weren't thinking. We were compelled by a force more powerful even than self-preservation. It was madness. And it was wonderful.

Tom leaves in a hurry, and I dive for the telephone.

21. THE MURDER

Thursday, 6:02 p.m. New Jersey

Jimmy Branford is already tired, highballing his way down the northern extension of the New Jersey Turnpike on his way to Elizabeth, NJ. He has been driving his empty flatbed from Buffalo most of the day. He stopped in Syracuse for a little nap in the cot behind the seats, but slept less than two hours before the alarm went off. Then he went into the all-night truck stop diner for coffee and a pancake lunch. He plans is to get to the dock in Elizabeth and get a good place in line, get dinner in the trucker's diner at the dock and then sleep the rest of the night. The container ship is scheduled to begin unloading at 6:00 a.m., and Jimmy wants to pick up his container as soon as possible so he can be back in Buffalo for dinner with the missus and his kids Friday night.

Hours fly by, and he sees the sign for the Vince Lombardi rest area and checks his watch. He has got time for a quick pee and then on to Elizabeth. He will be there by 8:00 p.m., and that should nail him an early spot in the RoRo lineup. He pulls in to Vince's Place, as he calls it, and parks as close as he can get to the door.

He rushes inside to the men's room. When he is done, he hurries back out, takes a deep breath of what passes for fresh air and smells something unpleasant drifting in from the east on a light breeze. It must be the slaughterhouses in Kearney, he says to himself, remembering the days when he used to drive meat carcasses up to Buffalo. It was harder work than ferrying containers up from Elizabeth. Those sides of beef were heavy.

He walks around his truck to check the tires before he starts off for the last, short leg. Force of habit. Everything looks good. He climbs up into the cab and starts the engine. Something sharp cuts into his neck, and he feels enormous pressure on his throat. He cannot breathe. Yusef is behind him out of sight. Jimmy struggles hard, but he cannot get his fingers under the wire, and he cannot reach back far enough with his arms to grab or hit the guy. In five minutes, his face is purple, and his tongue lolls out of his mouth, and the struggle is over. There is no sound. Too late, he thinks of sounding the air horn, which might have brought someone running, but he has spent his last few minutes trying to hit the guy behind him. He never saw the guy, who had ducked down low behind the seatback and was out of reach. He never even knew there was a second guy, Hussein, who could have taken over if Yusef had failed. Jimmy never had a chance.

The two killers pull his body over the seatback. Jimmy's head hits the floor first, and the weight of his body falling on it breaks his neck, although it does not matter at that point, but the two killers now sitting in the front seat hear the crack. Jimmy's torso topples over, and the legs follow in an awkward heap, squeezed into the small space. It is an ignominious way for anyone to die, but respect for the dead is not something the two are concerned with.

They drive the truck to the far end of the nearly empty parking lot, and no one sees the two men carry the body a few feet into the woods and dump it in the bushes. Back in the truck, the papers that will allow them to pick up the container are easy to find. They replace them with their own papers. For their next task, they have to get to a more secluded area. Back on the Turnpike, they head farther south past the Elizabeth exit, but that does not matter. After they have painted the truck cowling, they will turn around and head north again.

They pull into the Thomas Edison service area lot and park at the far back side. While Husain changes the license plates, Yusef climbs up on the roof with a can of ship's bottom red lead, nautical antifouling paint, which they have been specifically instructed to paint on the cowling. They believe it will protect their cargo from discovery as they enter New York City. A few truckers see them painting the cowling, but small maintenance jobs are often done on the road. It is a little unusual, but truckers are independent and rarely question the behavior of others. Besides, there will not be any reports of a missing truck for some time.

They do not bother to let the paint dry. They know it will collect insects and debris as they drive along, but that does not matter. The red paint is not there for looks but to protect them, so they think, from the prying laser beams of the New York police. They drive to the entrance of the northbound side of the Turnpike and drive back to the Vince Lombardi rest area where they killed the driver. They are sure no one saw them dumping the body, so they feel quite safe, parked on the other side and with the newly painted red cowling and the new license plates.

They find two hookers and take them quickly from behind. Killing Jimmy seems to have cranked up their libidos. After the hookers leave, they go to sleep, but they do not sleep well. Their Al Qaeda indoctrination — the Americans are crusaders, the West is evil — failed to erase their earlier religious instruction from their parents and hometown mullahs. A deep part of their conscience knows killing innocent people is wrong. The indoctrination makes it possible for them to do the deed, but it does not let them sleep peacefully afterwards. They are not rested in the morning when it is time to pick up their cargo.

22. THE COWLING

Thursday, 7:30 p.m, Washington D.C.

"Colonel Haldane's office." It's late, but Edward's there. This time his voice doesn't affect me. It's the same velvet sound, but it doesn't move me. It takes me only a second to realize I'm the one who's changed. I'm just not horny anymore. Not for Edward, anyway. The Eagles got it right, as they did so many things, I think — "You're not the same old gal you used to be." Then I remember the song a little better — oh yeah, it says "You're still the same old gal you used to be." Well, they got a lot of other things right.

"Hi, Edward. This is Kimmie Hansen with the *Times*. Is the colonel in?"

"Yes, Ms. Hansen. I'll put you right through."

"Hi, Kimmie, how's your father doing?" I hesitate for a second then realize her phone, once secure, must have been tapped.

"Well, frankly, Colonel, he's been better. That show he's in is going to open soon, but we don't know exactly when." I feel a little silly using this spy-speak stuff, but I know it's necessary.

"Oh, I see. Will you know about it soon?"

"No, I don't think so. Not exactly. Probably we'll be able to narrow it down a little, but that's all. But we know the actors, and we know the plot, so we've got that to go on. I called to tell you about it. They're painting the scenery now."

"Oh. What color would they be painting it now?" She's speaking in an Irish brogue to me. Just to goof around, I guess. Anyone who can goof around when there are impending death and destruction has my undying admiration.

"They're painting it that funny red color you like so much. Not the black."

"Great. That sounds just right to me."

"I'm glad to hear it, Colonel. You going to be able to take care of things at your end?"

"I sure will. Are you going to need any help, d'you think, what with the play and all?"

"I don't think so, but that's my friend Tom's department. I'll give him your number."

"Do that. I may be persona non grata around here, but I still pull a little weight where it counts, and I can get some of the troops up there for the show if you want. Or any kind of experts." She finished a speech that was long for her.

"I'll tell Tom."

"OK, well, good luck."

"If you wouldn't mind sitting on that information for a few days, that'd be helpful. The red scenery's going to be particularly nice for us."

"Oh sure. I understand. I won't do anything that'll interfere. I can do what I need to without bothering you."

"Thanks. We'll talk." I wonder what she's going to do. As long as the mole doesn't get any information to send back "home," there won't be any harm in leaving him in place. The only information that could get in our way is the fact that we're bugging the apartment. And it looks as though that operation's pretty much over too. Of course, we still have the cell-phone tap. And the computer.

***

I log on. It's the usual string of notes about relatives — "Aunt Sara is well, as is Uncle George. Everyone is having a fine vacation. Too bad it will end in just a short while." Nothing that's helpful.

I call Tom. I know he'd have gone back to the office.

"Have you talked to the director?"

"Yes. He's talking to the governor right now, but it doesn't look good. We don't have enough solid information to take such a drastic step. I can imagine the governor's uncertainties. It'd cost a lot of people a lot of money, millions probably."

"But the risk is to destroy a lot of the city." I raise my voice more than a few decibels.

"You don't need to convince me."

"I know. It's just frustrating."

"I've got the ship narrowed down."

"Tell me."

"There's one arriving tonight — the *Rodina*, out of St. Petersburg via Rotterdam. Then nothing tomorrow, then two on Wednesday, one out of Le Havre and one out of Gdansk. There's another one due in on Thursday, but that's as far as they go, and our boat's probably going to come in before that anyway. They'll be another set of arrivals published tomorrow around three o'clock."

"What d'you think?" I get that urge to cross my fingers again.

"I hate to say it, but my bet'd be on the *Rodina*, arriving tonight." He sounds grim.

"Oh, shit. We might be too late already."

"I sent two guys down to Elizabeth to take a look. They're watching the RoRo lineup — the trucks waiting to go on the ship to pick up containers. They're looking for the red cowling."

"That's hopeful." I wonder if I'm grasping at straws.

"Maybe, but it's hard to spot at night. The guys tell me all the dark colors look alike unless they're right under a floodlight."

"Is there any other bad news?"

"No, but I also have the New Jersey and the New York state troopers watching all the bridges and tunnels, and a special alert on the George Washington Bridge."

"And they're looking for the red cowling?"

"Yes. It's our main piece of information." He doesn't sound discouraged, but I'm alarmed everything now is hanging on the color of the truck's cowling. We need to know when the ship's coming in. The cops could turn it around and head it back out to sea.

"D'you have anything?"

"I called Colonel Haldane and told her about the red cowling."

"That doesn't help us with our current situation."

"I know, but she offered military assistance."

"That might be useful." I give him her number.

"I think you should move out of the apartment. The veep's guys are gonna take another swipe at you."

"Oh, Jesus. I hadn't even thought about it."

"I can tell you *they're* thinking about it. The goons who're doing it are going to want to finish the job so they can get paid. They've tried twice now. Didn't you say you had a friend in the building?"

"Sure. Judy. The one who tipped me off to this apartment."

"Move in with Judy." He says this like an order, and I feel a little tingle. I didn't know I would respond like that to strength in a man. I hope we get through this, I think, so I can get in bed with Tom again. I shake the thought off like dewdrops in my hair. This is no time to be distracted.

"OK." I have that same feeling of submissiveness.

"That way you can still monitor their cell phones and computer. What's Judy's apartment number and phone number?

I want to be able to reach you."

I like hearing that, and I give him the numbers after looking them up in my date book. Of course I haven't checked with Judy yet, but if she can't take me in, I'll figure out another solution and get back to Tom.

"I'm not tying up your line, am I?"

"I've got a lot of lines here. It's the New York office after all. If something happens I'll hear. But I want you to move to Judy's as soon as you can."

"OK, I'll move."

I call Judy. She's asleep. I look at my watch. It's just past midnight. I can't believe so much time has passed. Judy's a little surprised, but she knows about the whistleblower story and the explosion in my old apartment, and when I tell her about the gunshot, she offers to help.

I get my stuff together. I put Gaylord's receivers into a plastic shopping bag and take them without turning them off. I have to make several trips, even without all my stuff. It's after 2:00 in the morning when we're done, and Judy shows me the couch, gets some bedclothes, and I fall asleep the moment my body is horizontal.

Cargo

23. AL AND MUHAMMAD

Thursday. New York City

When the meeting of the cell on 81st St. breaks up, Al Akhbar and Muhammad Al Aksa go home and start packing. There is nothing more for them to do. They are lucky to find seats on a flight that night to Amsterdam, where they figure they will get a plane to one of the Arabic countries without anyone even noticing. They estimate during the second leg of their two-stage flight — while they are en route to Riyadh or Damascus — the bomb will go off in New York, and they figure will seriously distract everyone.

So they check in at the KLM desk, each of them carrying one of the blue gym bags Becca bought for everyone. Inside the bags, they have each wrapped up a handgun in tinfoil so it will not rattle, then stuffed it in the mouth of a musical instrument — Al carries a French horn and Muhammad a saxophone. When they go through the security gate, their instruments show up looking completely innocent on the X-ray monitor. The men are just two Saudi musicians who have visited the States to learn about American jazz.

They do not know, and they are fortunate none of the security officers know, the French horn is about as unlikely a jazz instrument as an Irish harp. Once through the security gate, they begin to relax. They amble down the corridor, dangling their instrument cases in one hand and the blue gym bags in the other.

At the KLM gate sitting area, however, they start to feel nervous again. There are so many people, and the two Arabs with instruments stand out. They try not to let their nervousness show. They keep telling themselves everything is going to be OK, but that seems to make them more nervous. They do not want to sweat, but how do you keep yourself from sweating? They are armed, and if police officers start to approach them, they will open their instrument cases, unwrap the handguns, and force their way onto a plane and then to some anti-U.S. airport — Havana, Cuba, probably. But nothing like that happens.

They try to look relaxed, reading newspapers, eating hot dogs. They have developed an enormous appetite for hot dogs while they were in America, and they want to enjoy them as much as they can before they get home. They know in the back of their minds it is the pork in the hot dogs that makes them taste so good, but they never say anything about it and are very careful not to read the labels on the hot dog box. They have gone out to bars and drunk at least once a week and thought nothing of it. And they have gone to some very high-class whorehouses in New York. These too are sins in the religion they are fighting for, but most of the Muslims they know pay little attention to these prohibitions. It is as if the sins of drinking alcohol and fornicating are minor compared to the sin of eating pork. The latter they cannot admit even to themselves, and certainly not to each other. So they just marvel at how delicious American hot dogs are and eat three each for lunch at the airport. Before their flight is announced, they go back to the lunch stand and have another one each.

The announcement comes on time, and they stand in line with the small crowd — a mixture of Dutch citizens and American tourists. The two Muslims smile a little at each other as if to say "we're getting away with it." The ground crew announces the sections of the airplane that should board, and it does not take long before their section is called. They check their boarding passes to make sure and head for the gate.

The gatekeeper takes their boarding passes, and they enter the long corridor, sloping down to the plane. Each time they go successfully through a stage of their escape, they feel more relief. Then, as the next stage approaches, they start to feel anxious again. The anxiety does not help their digestion, which is already dealing with four hot dogs.

On the plane they find their seats and store their musical instruments in the overhead compartments as they were told to. The horn case barely fits, but with a little pushing it goes in. The saxophone is easy. They sit down. As they wait for the plane to pull away from the gate, their anxiety levels rise again. The plane seems to wait, motionless, at the gate for a very long time, longer than necessary. But eventually the flight attendant closes the door, and the plane is towed away from the gate and turned. The engines rev just a little, and the pilot taxies the big plane to a position in a line of planes waiting for clearance. The two terrorists are still not relaxed. They know if they are uncovered through some search of the passenger lists, the plane can be easily turned around and brought back to the gate under heavy security.

But nothing happens. The plane takes off, reaches its cruising altitude, and the flight attendants come around soliciting orders for drinks. After the second cocktail and the lunch of airline food, which they both pronounce quite excellent, they begin to relax. They are on their way, well out over the Atlantic.

They do not know it, but Tom has sent out a standard be-on-the-lookout bulletin to all the airports in the New York area. The bulletin arrives at the KLM check-in counter an hour after the plane has taken off. The ticketing agent remembers the two men — they used their real names and fit the descriptions perfectly — and calls the number given on the bulletin to report they are flying on KLM 457 to Amsterdam and are due to arrive at Schiphol Airport at 8:00 a.m. Dutch time the next morning. The New York Interpol liaison calls his Dutch counterpart, and arrangements are made to "greet" the terrorists when they arrive in Amsterdam. The arrangements take only a few phone calls to the KLM security team, who in turn call the pilot and the airport authorities, and within 30 minutes, everything is ready. A plan for just such an eventuality was formulated years before and refined during several simulations. Everyone knows what they are supposed to do.

The plane lands on schedule but taxies to a place far away from regular traffic. The pilot goes on the intercom and explains they will have to sit there for a while to wait for an arrival gate to be cleared. As soon as the plane stops, twelve Dutch security officers, ten men and two women, approach the plane from the side that Muhammad and Al cannot see. Entering from the rear door, half of them stay in the rear. The other six walk through the luggage compartment to the front of the plane. Two of the men and two of the women wear flight attendant uniforms. The captain goes on the intercom again and sounding as weary as he knows his passengers are feeling, tells them sympathetically that the wait will be a little longer and that, meanwhile, the cabin crew will offer them drinks and snacks to help them put up with the delay. Al and Muhammad feel they are very close to being on their flight home and are unconcerned.

Two of the security officers dressed as flight attendants approach the seats where the terrorists are sitting. They make sure the overhead compartments are still closed. Two more security officers dressed as flight attendants come up the aisle from the rear. One of them speaks to the couple sitting behind Al and Muhammad and tells them they will have to come back to the rear of the plane because there is a problem with their entry forms. The couple, complaining, get up and leave. As soon as their seats are vacant, one of the "flight attendants" asks Al and Muhammad what they would like to drink, and during this small distraction, the other two slip into the seats behind them and flip leather belts over the two men's heads, pulling them back against the headrests. Because they are still belted in, they can hardly move. They wave their arms helplessly until the security agents in front have them handcuffed. The arrest takes less than a minute.

Once they are cuffed, leg shackles are attached to their feet. Once shackled, their seatbelts are undone and the men pulled to their feet and led, shuffling, to the rear of the plane, out the door and down the steps — carefully so they do not trip on their leg shackles. Once on the tarmac, they are stuffed, gently but unceremoniously, into a waiting police van. The security officers who remained behind retrieve the musical instruments and the two gym bags. Then they too leave by the rear door.

The pilot comes on the intercom. "We do not always offer our passengers additional drama," he says. "Most of them think the movies are bad enough."

Passengers chuckle nervously and look around.

"We have just removed two dangerous criminals from the plane. They will be flown back to New York, where they will be taken care of. Thank you to the airport security detail. As always a thoroughly professional job."

Some of the passengers clap. Others seem to be a little worried. Could there be some others on board that escaped detection? Everyone starts talking at once. Then the plane moves toward the gate.

Al and Muhammad are taken to a high security holding cell in the airport while a police plane is readied. In an hour they are flying back toward New York City, and now they are beginning to be very nervous. They are pretty sure the plane will not land at New York. They think probably there will not even be a New York. The plane will probably be diverted, and there will surely be a lot of confusion. There might be a chance for them to get away.

24. ARRIVAL

Friday, 7:00 a.m. New Jersey

Captain Zhakdin settles into his chair on the bridge, orders his breakfast of tea and bread, and looks thoughtfully at the horizon. In a few minutes, the sun will make its dramatic appearance, and he will remember the dreams he had about the sea, now fulfilled.

The trip has been uneventful except for the storm that caused an engine failure and the anomaly that was discovered the next day. These events are behind him now, and he is unconcerned.

He instructs the ship's communications officer to call the port of Elizabeth and announce his imminent arrival. He calls the engine room and orders them to slow the engines as the ship enters a heavily trafficked shipping lane. He sips his tea thoughtfully and nibbles on the bread. In a minute he hears the engines slow down and feels a change in the vibrations that permeate the ship. The engine room calls back

"Engines at half-full, Captain."

"Very good."

He instructs the communications officer to place a private call to his wife. It is late at night in the town outside Moscow where he lives, and he apologizes to his wife for the call. She welcomes his call with less enthusiasm than usual.

"We are approaching Elizabeth," he says.

"I thought you were going to New York," she says.

"Elizabeth is close to New York," he tells her.

"Will you have time go into the city?" she asks.

"I do not know yet. Probably not. Is there something you

would like?"

"Yes. A magazine about the movie stars."

"I cannot make a special trip for that, but there will be a newsstand in the port area."

"Good. I would like to read about them."

He thinks his wife's interests in movie stars is trivial, but he says nothing.

"Where are you going next?" she asks.

"We have to stand off and wait for some trucks to arrive. Then we head for Spain."

"That will be nice for you," she says with a touch of sarcasm.

"Yes. Warmer temperatures will be welcome."

His breakfast dishes are taken away, and he runs his morning check over the ship's systems. As they get closer to the port, a pilot will be sent out to board the ship, and Zhakdin instructs the crew to prepare for the pilot's arrival.

A half hour elapses, and he asks the engine room to slow the engines even more as he sees a launch arriving with the pilot. The pilot comes on board and heads for the bridge where Captain Zhakdin greets him graciously and formally turns the ship over to him and issues instructions for the crew to prepare for docking. As is his custom, the captain stays on the bridge. He looks around as other ships come into view. He dislikes having the ship under the pilot's control but has no choice in the matter. Finally they receive their assignment and Captain Zhakdin orders the crew to make ready for docking. Two tugs approach and tow the ship toward its assigned dock.

When all the lines are deployed and the huge ship brought to a complete standstill, the ramps are lowered. The trucks drive up the ramps, ready to receive their assigned containers. The crane moves across the ship, picking up containers as the crew swarms over each one, unlocking the straps that hold them in place, and attaching the hoist. The dirty yellow container is lifted, craned over to the waiting truck with the two drivers and the dark-red cowling, lowered into position, and locked down. The drivers exit down the ramp and head to the highway and the George Washington Bridge.

25. AT THE BRIDGE

Friday, Early Morning. New York City

I wake up to the light coming in the window. I've gotten five hours of sleep. It's not enough. In the bathroom I look in the mirror and feel like screaming. I look awful. There's a famous painting called *The Scream*, with a person — you can't even tell if it's a man or woman — screaming with both hands held up to his or her face. That's how I feel.

My receiver is still turned on, and if anything's been said, I know I'd have been instantly awake. I wake Judy up apologetically and tell her I have one more load to get and could she listen to the receiver and tell me anything she hears while I go back up for the last of my stuff. She yawns and nods. She knows it's important, but she thinks it's about my safety. She has no idea about the bomb.

When I come back to Judy's apartment with my last pair of garbage bags full of shoes and boots, Judy's sleeping in the big living room chair in her bathrobe and slippers. The receiver's in her lap.

"Did you hear anything?" I wake her up with a jolt.

"Yes." She rubs her eyes and clears her throat. "There was one call just a few minutes ago. A man's voice. He had an accent. He said, 'We're loaded, waiting for traffic to clear, then we'll be on the Turnpike.'"

"Oh, my God." I'm horrorstruck. "They've gotten through. What did the other person say?"

"It was a woman. I didn't hear everything, but I heard the words 'Plan A.'"

"Oh, shit!" They keep getting ahead of us.

"What is it?" Judy's getting alarmed. "Are they coming after you? They don't know you're here, do they?"

"No. I'm safe for the time being, but there's another problem I can't tell you about."

She looks a little sulky at not being let in on the secret, but reporters do have to keep secrets, and I guess she imagines it's some story I'm working on. I don't have time to worry about what she thinks.

"You might as well go back to bed. We're OK, and there's nothing more to do." I want to tell her to get out of the city, but I know that would be a mistake.

She nods, half asleep, and trundles off to her bedroom, scuffing her slippers as she walks away. I hear her crash onto the bed in the other room. She's going to be late for work.

I call Tom.

"They're loaded up and waiting to get on the Turnpike!" I whisper as loudly as I can, trying to convey the disaster to him without waking Judy up.

"OK, let's keep calm. Hang on just a minute." I hear him put me on hold, and I start to go into a boil. Doesn't he know how serious this is?

"Hi, Kimmie. Sorry for the interruption. What else d'you know?"

I tell him about Judy listening for a while and what she said.

"Shouldn't we get some people up there to stop them?" I think my anger's showing through in my voice.

"Take it easy. I did that already. While you were on hold."

I feel my whole body relax. He really does know what he's doing.

"Are you moved in?"

"Yes, all of my stuff's out of the old place."

"OK. Then we're as much in control as we can be."

That seems an unnecessarily fatalistic point of view, but I'm not going to start talking philosophy at this point.

"I'm going up there." I mean the George Washington Bridge.

"OK." He knows not to try to stop me. "I'll call and tell them who you are in case you get there first. Bring your cell-phone-tap gizmo with you. You'll be able to hear them if they talk. That might help us. I'll meet you there — the headquarters building on the New Jersey side, where the 9W overpass is."

"Sure. I know the place." I want to tell him how I feel, but I realize how inappropriate it is when we're bracing ourselves against this attack. I say goodbye and hang up.

I get the receiver from where Judy'd dropped it on the chair. I listen at her door and hear her snoring. The poor girl hasn't a clue about what's happening, and I know I can't tell her. She'd have to tell someone she loved, like her mother, and her mother would have to tell someone else, and before the morning was half over, everyone in New York would know what was going on, and there'd be a general panic, and people would get hurt. It's better if I just do what I can to help stop them getting into the city. And what's that, I ask myself? Not much, but I do have my receiver. I'll hear them talking to each other.

Outside, I hail a cab. "George Washington Bridge. New Jersey side. And step on it." I show him a wad of money. He doesn't hesitate for a second.

We charge up the West Side Highway and over the bridge. He lets me off at the bus stop under the overpass for Route 9W, and I get out and run up the stairs.

The headquarters building is on the south side of the highway below me. I run over the bridge and cross a few busy roads. Inside the headquarters building, I ask where the state troopers are that the New York FBI office requested. It's like going into a restaurant and asking the maître d' for the Smith party, only more serious. The Port Authority officer directs me up a flight of stairs. There's a door at the top that opens into a big room, where I see a bunch of uniformed New Jersey state troopers, and some others not in uniform. They're all looking out a large window that gives them a view of the whole approach to the tollbooths on the upper level. On the wall above their heads, there's a big clock. It's 8:32.

"Who's in charge of the group the FBI requested?"

A young plainclothes guy turns and identifies himself. I try to smile.

"I'm Kimmie Hansen from the *Times*."

"Yes, ma'am. Tom Shipman called to say you'd be here. He said you had a tap on their cell phone. I'm Lieutenant Garmaine."

"Hi," I say, but I'm very focused and don't really take him in. He's young though. I can see that, and I wonder if he's had enough experience to handle something this big.

I take out my device. It's still tuned to the preset frequency. There's nothing. We listen for a while, then I set the device down, leaving it on.

"If they place a call, we'll hear it. What's the setup?" I look out at the line of tollbooths that stretch across the 12 lanes of the eastbound highway. The westbound side's been free for many years, and the traffic over there is zooming by. That's good, I think, the more people get out of the city the better. Then I see all the cars lining up to pay tolls and go into the city. I want to shout to them to turn around and go back.

"I've got a man in every tollbooth on this level." The young trooper is explaining it all to me. "There are also several men on the lower level, just in case. They're all looking for a semi with a dark-red cowling, pulling a shipping container. We should be able to see it from here too, if they use the upper level."

"They planned to use the upper level."

There are 12 tollbooths, and all of them are open. I can see there's an extra person in each one, and I can imagine the additional person is heavily armed. I look down the road and find the approach that comes from Route 95. I point.

"That's where they'll be coming from."

"Yes, ma'am. Unless they change their plans or get a little lost. It's a pretty confusing approach if you haven't done it before."

That's a point I hadn't thought of — that they might get lost. They might take the lower level by mistake, or get off and end up in the streets of Fort Lee. There are just too many variables for me to feel comfortable.

Tom arrives a few minutes later. He gives me a big hug, but then goes right to work checking out the setup, and I hear the trooper telling him the same things he told me.

The receiver suddenly crackles, and I hear a male voice say, "We're getting close to the George Washington Bridge." Tom hears it too and tells the plainclothesman who then mutters something I can't hear into his communicator.

"There they are!" All of us in the observation area spot the red cowling at the same time. The container is a dirty yellow. As they get closer, we can see they're keeping to the right, staying in the slow lane. The young, plainclothes trooper says something into his communicator. It doesn't matter that I can't hear what he's saying. There's only one thing he could be saying.

In a few seconds, it becomes clear which lane they're heading for — the second tollbooth, close to us. The trooper says something again. Everyone's ready and alert. The reporter in me looks up at the clock. It's 8:44. Tom is standing right next to me, so close I can feel the tension in his body.

As the truck starts to slow down — there are four cars ahead of it at tollbooth number two — Lieutenant Garmaine barks an order into his communicator. It's a code word, so I don't get the meaning of it right away, but I can see the armed men in the tollbooths stepping outside and getting their weapons off their shoulders and into their hands. But they aren't pointing them at anyone yet.

The truck is only a few yards from the first car in the line when the drivers realize there are armed men coming out of the tollbooths, focused on them. Suddenly the truck pulls sharply to the right out of the lineup and accelerates. For a minute they're heading right toward us, but they continue swerving until they're angling back a little. Maybe they're going to try to go back the way they came, against the traffic. I know that won't work for them, but I feel a surge of gladness that maybe we've kept them out of Manhattan. Then I think how destructive the weapon they're carrying is, and I know the danger's not over.

As the truck turns, I see the driver hunch forward close up against the wheel, and the guy in the passenger's seat push behind his back and poke a gun barrel out the window.

Immediately, the crackling sound of automatic gunfire fills the air. The toll taker in the number two tollbooth disappears out of sight. There are bullet holes in the glass of her tollbooth, but there's no way to know if she's been hit or has ducked down for cover.

The truck keeps accelerating, and I see where they're headed. There's a one-lane exit ramp where a driver can turn off to go talk to the tollbooth officials to get an E-ZPass or something. It's the last exit from the bridge, and it leads to the local roads. The truck bounces over a curb, and we all wince, remembering the cargo's susceptible to detonation if it's jounced around too much.

But nothing happens.

In only a few seconds, the truck's gotten onto the single lane exit and heads for the local roads of Fort Lee. On the bridge there's pandemonium. At the sound of the gunfire, some drivers jump out of their cars and dive for the pavement. Others duck down behind their dashboards. Toll takers crouch down behind the walls of the booths. The armed officers run out of the booths, trying to chase after the accelerating truck, but I notice none of them fires at it.

Several officers kneel by one who's been shot. They're talking into their communicators, calling for medical assistance, I'm sure. Several civilian cars, those about to pay their tolls, step on their accelerators and break through the flimsy wooden barriers and rocket away over the bridge. Who could blame them?

There's a police chase car stationed on the bridge side of the tolls, off to the right, and the officer driving it makes a U-turn and turns on his siren. He tries to get through the toll lanes, but they're badly blocked by cars, most of which have been abandoned by their drivers and can't be moved. The chase car backs up and looks for another lane. Eventually he finds lane number eight is possible, and he worms his way through it, siren wailing uselessly. But by that time, the truck's long gone and out of sight.

***

Tom and I and the trooper in charge dash for the door and run down the stairs. In the lot are several police cars. The trooper opens one, and we all pile in. I get in the front seat, which means Tom has to go in back. I'm the one with the listening device, and I think it'll be important for me to see as much as possible.

We fly out of the parking lot and down the exit ramp then turn south on River Rd. It's the most direct route south from the bridge, running along the river. The lieutenant reaches down and switches on his siren then glances at me.

"We're going to be driving fast. I hope you don't mind."

"Not at all. Let's get there." Could there be anything more important, I wonder.

We pick up speed, passing cars that've pulled over in response to our siren, slowing just enough at intersections to make sure the coast is clear, then accelerating to the street beyond. Past the driver's shoulder, I can see Manhattan. I wonder if it'll still be there in a couple of hours.

I suddenly think of Gaylord. I don't want him to be incinerated. In a way, he represents New York, at least something that New York has, one of its qualities — zany creativity. It should be preserved. Of course that's silly thinking. There are zanily creative people outside of New York, but they're not exactly like Gaylord. Well, no one is. Probably I'm just rationalizing, but it doesn't matter. I still want Gaylord out of the city, but I can't tell him why.

The other problem is I don't dare use my cell phone because a call from any one of the cell members might reveal some critical piece of information. I squirm around to Tom and yell.

"D'you have your cell phone?"

"Yes, but don't try to warn anyone. It'll cause a terrible panic."

"I know that. I'm not going to say anything about the bomb, but I want to get a friend of mine out of the city. I won't tell him why."

"OK." He reaches in his shirt pocket for a cell phone and hands it to me.

"Thanks." I realize he's trusting me with vital information.

I dial Gaylord's store, and he answers. I start thinking as fast as I can.

"Listen, Gaylord, I want to ask you something. It's an invitation actually."

"Mmm, that sounds intriguing."

"I can promise you much more than intrigue. It's going to be the most exciting thing that's ever happened to you. I'm having a party in, in Poughkeepsie. I know, I know, why Poughkeepsie? That's part of the surprise. You should leave the city right away. Don't pack. You won't need any clothes. Everything you need will be supplied." I'm babbling, I know, but I'm trying to find the right button to propel Gaylord out of the city. "Don't waste any time. Just rent a car and drive to Poughkeepsie as fast as you can."

"Where's this party going to be? I mean, where in Poughkeepsie, sweet thing?"

I couldn't think of anything to tell him. "When you get to Poughkeepsie, you'll see signs. We're taking over the whole town. You'll know where to go. But don't wait. Leave now."

As I say this, I see the lieutenant look at me, and his hand moves a little. If I'd started to say anything more, he'd have snatched the cell phone from me.

Gaylord's voice interrupts this little drama. "You're not joking, are you?"

"No, I'm not joking. Don't say anything to anyone. Not everyone's invited. Just leave. Like I said, drive to Poughkeepsie as fast as you can."

"OK. I'll go on this little adventure. Will you be there in Poughkeepsie?"

"No, not right away, but I'll talk to you later."

"OK."

"Bye."

We hang up, and I hand the phone back to Tom. "Thanks," I say too softly, given the noise. I want to tell him how much I appreciate his trust. But instead I tell him, "Gaylord's a very smart man with an insatiable curiosity about life, and I'm pretty sure he'll do exactly as I said."

"I hope so. There isn't much time."

My phone buzzes, which signals that the terrorists' frequency is active. I push the green button and jam the phone to my ear, hoping to hear something that'll tell me where the truck is.

It's one of the drivers. "They had the bridge blocked already. We're headed south away from the bridge."

"How'd they know you were coming over the bridge?" It's Becca.

"I don't know. Maybe they have guards everywhere."

"Maybe, but I don't think so. Did they recognize the truck somehow?"

"Yes. They came out with guns as soon as we approached."

"Maybe the special paint on the cowling doesn't work as well as we were told."

"I don't know." The driver sounds distracted, and I can imagine him driving along in an area he doesn't know very well, worrying about the police, checking his mirrors often and trying to talk to Becca at the same time.

"Of course, the paint itself would tell them even quicker. Damn! We should have thought of that." Becca's pissed, and I'm glad. She suddenly sounds a little less sure of herself, like she doesn't know exactly what trick we played or who to trust. I'm only just beginning to realize we're lucky the mole was the one connected to the red cowling. If it were either of the other two guys, we wouldn't have a clue about the truck carrying the bomb.

"What should we do?" It's the driver or his partner, still

talking to Becca. I guess they've left the line open, which makes sense for them.

"Keep heading south. That's good. Head for Hoboken. Plan C."

I hear the phone click. The connection's been broken. Probably Becca broke it. She suddenly has a lot to do, like get the hell out of Dodge. Or maybe she realizes we might be listening.

I turn and lean so Tom and the trooper can hear me.

"They're headed for Hoboken."

"Did they say what route they're taking?"

"No. Nothing about the route. Just south."

The trooper speaks into his communicator. I can't hear everything, but I do hear him give a description of the truck. Police units in the NJ area between the George Washington Bridge and the Holland Tunnel should be looking.

"How many routes to Hoboken are there from here?" I ask the trooper.

"Three obvious ones. But there are some smaller roads they could use to switch from one route to another. One of the police units should spot them pretty soon."

"I hope so."

Then there's silence from the radio. The trooper's driving fast, heading south on what he thinks is the most likely route the truck would take. Despite all the motion, and the noise of the police siren, it feels still and silent as we drive along. "Silent" because it's the sound of the cell-phone monitor we're listening for, and "still" even though we're bouncing around and jerking back and forth, we haven't come up to the truck. So the three of us are waiting tensely for something to happen, either a call-in from a police car that the truck's been spotted or another call between Becca and the drivers.

The phone buzzes again.

"Hello?" Becca's answering. I've got the phone jammed up against my ear, hoping the drivers'll say something about where they are.

"It's Nat." Damn. This is no time for chit-chat.

"What's the situation?" he asks.

"They had the bridge staked out." She's yelling, and I hear loud motor sounds. "The guys got away and are heading for Hoboken."

"Plan C?" Nat asks.

"Yes. Where are you?"

"On the East River, near the UN."

"You know where to go — up the East River, through Hell's Gate and into Long Island Sound. But step on it. I'll tell you when the timer's been set so you'll know the exact time of detonation. You don't want to be on the water when it goes off. So head for a harbor as soon as you get into Long Island Sound. Steal a car. You'll get farther away."

"I remember."

I can see she doesn't think he's too bright. They've been over the plan before.

I tell Tom and the lieutenant where he's going.

"What kind of boat does he have?" the lieutenant asks.

"I don't know. They said it'd be fast."

"And what's the guy like who's driving it?"

"He's around six feet tall, white, speaks English, American, brown hair."

"And he's alone in the boat?" The lieutenant's obviously interested in catching the guy.

"I think so." I begin to wonder what Al and Muhammad did to get out of the city. They could have left a long time ago. Their jobs were done. The trooper speaks again.

"Is he armed?"

"Yes."

"There are six people altogether." I have to shout over the siren. "Nat, who's in the boat. Becca, who's in another boat on the Hudson, and she's making the decisions. The two drivers in the truck – Yusef and Hussein. And there are two other guys – Al and Muhammad."

"Where are they?"

"I don't know. Their job was to gather information on the power supply and on the bus and subway system, and that job was done when the group met last night for the last time. They could've left the city after that."

"What else d'you know about them? Wait a second." He negotiates an intersection, making sure the coast is clear before he crosses.

"Al worked for Con Ed, and Muhammad worked for the Port Authority. They lived on 82nd St." I fish in my purse for my planner, where I wrote their address and phone number down.

"Not now," he says. "You've given me enough. They're Arabic-looking, I assume, from the names?"

"Yes. Al is big, strong looking, and I'd guess very cool in a tight spot. Muhammad's smaller and more nervous." I have to shout.

He speaks into his communicator again, and I assume he's calling headquarters to have an alert sent out. Those two guys could be out of the country by now.

"OK." He puts his communicator back on his belt. "I've asked headquarters to alert the coast guard about the two boats, and to notify the airports, car rentals, and trains about Al and Muhammad."

Tom nods vigorously in approval. "Anything else you can think of?"

229

"Yes. The drivers said that after they parked the truck — if it was going to be in Hoboken —they'd steal a car and drive to Chicago. I think probably there's another cell in Chicago they plan to hook up with."

"That's helpful." He calls on his communicator again. The Chicago police are going to be warned about the cell.

"I have all these conversations recorded. So you can go over them with a fine-toothed comb, if…" I let my voice trail off.

"Yeah. There's that big if." Tom looks glum.

The phone buzzes again. It's Becca's phone. I hear her answer. "Hello?"

"Hi, Becca. It's Yusef. We're in Weehawken, and I see some docks over to the left, on the river. I think we should park it and take off. They'll spot us soon."

"OK. Go ahead. Tell Hussein to set the detonator now."

Oh damn. I'd hoped the truck would be stopped before they set the detonator.

"Yes. He'll do it."

The connection is broken. I tell Tom and the trooper they're going to park the truck at the Weehawken docks and that they're setting the detonator. The trooper grabs his communicator and makes a call. I hear him barking orders to a bomb-squad person. He turns to me.

"D'you know how much time is on the detonator?"

"They planned to put an hour on it. They have to get far away." I'm still shouting.

"Right. That gives us plenty of time. I hope the detonator's a simple type. The bomb-squad guys are on their way by helicopter."

26. OUTING A MOLE

Friday, 9 a.m. Washington, D.C.

Col. Haldane taps her pencil thoughtfully on her desk and stares at her calendar. She knows what might or might not be happening in New York City. She is concerned about it, but she also believes the law enforcement officials in New York are very competent and will take care of it. Here in Washington, she thinks, she has her own problem to contend with — a mole in the Procurement Department. Under ordinary circumstances, the discovery of a spy amid any government operation would call for a very specific response on the part of the worker who made the discovery — inform the FBI and turn over all the information you have that suggests the guilt of the spy. When the government agency being spied on is a branch of the military, it is even more important to follow this procedure. Col. Haldane, however, wants none of that.

From the beginning, she has suspected the mole is one of three men who have been appointed by the vice president to their positions in her office. Her suspicion is grounded in the fact that when she uncovered malfeasance in her department and reported it to her superior officer, nothing was done. Her superior officer reported her discovery to one of the three men in question, and they (or he — it was never clear whether they were a team or three individual bureaucrats who shared loyalty to the vice president) simply sat on it, doing nothing. This made the colonel suspicious because they should have been concerned about the malfeasance. Of course, it could be merely greed on the vice president's part that resulted in these three cronies of his not wanting to rock a boat already loaded to the gunwales with gold bars. But it could also have been allegiance to a foreign power, or worse. Throughout government, people were beginning to realize the Islamic fundamentalist groups had spread themselves quite widely around the globe. Allegiance to one of the terrorist organizations might also be responsible for the inaction that followed her chain-of-command report.

But which one of the three men was it? By feeding a different story to each of them, and then waiting to see which of the three stories was mentioned by the cell members, the colonel identified the mole. Kimmie asked her, however, to wait for a while before acting so the New York police operation against the terrorists would not be compromised. Now enough time has passed, she thinks, and even though there is the possibility that New York will be destroyed within a few hours, she still has to act on the information she has. She hesitates, however, about going to the FBI. She is not sure whether the agency has also been infiltrated. There is some reason to believe it has. Certainly, the vice president's men, who have been placed in key positions all over the government, have infiltrated them. That, however, is more likely a strategy to make sure the vice president's company makes a great deal of money from the current wars in the Middle East or any natural disaster that comes along, than it is a part of a terrorist plot to attack major American cities. Still, she cannot be sure. Hard as it is to believe, it is possible the vice president is greedy enough to commit treason to fill his company's coffers even more than they already are.

It all comes down to the fact that she will have to act on her own.

She opens her word processor and types the following memo:

To: All Section Heads

From: Col. R.R. Haldane
Re: Espionage Activity

It came to my attention some time ago that there was a mole in the Procurement Department. Information from this department was shared quickly with a terrorist cell operating in New York City. I took it upon myself to identify the mole by supplying several different members of the Procurement Department with pieces of misinformation. The item that was then shared with the NYC cell made it evident that the mole is Mr. Clyde Jesperson, a civilian who was transferred to Procurement from the vice president's office some months ago. All departments are warned that information given to Mr. Jesperson can and will be shared with the country's enemies.

I am sure that Mr. Jesperson will complain and threaten me as a result of this memo, but I predict he will take no concrete action because to do so would only make his guilt more evident.

She then sends the memo via email to all the section heads in Procurement and to the director of counterespionage in the FBI.

Jesperson is in her doorway in ten minutes, sputtering and threatening her. "You cannot get away with this kind of character assassination," he says. "I will see you are dishonorably discharged, and I will sue you for defamation of character."

"Please do," she replies. "I will enjoy the process."

He blusters and fumes a little more before leaving. Col. Haldane smiles to herself and reaches for the phone.

"Edward, would you get Kimmie Hansen in New York?"

"Yes, ma'am," Edward answers.

A moment later Kimmie, a little breathless, answers the phone.

"Hello?"

"It's Roxie Haldane," she says.

My brain registers a very brief "Roxie?!" and then gets down to business.

"Colonel, we're in a very tight situation here, and I need to keep this line open."

"Understand. I just wanted you to know I've outed the mole here."

"OK," I say. "Thanks for waiting on it. Bye." I hang up as quickly as I can and check to see if I've missed any calls. I haven't.

27. YUSEF AND HUSSEIN

Friday, 11 a.m. New York City

The phone buzzes again, and I hear Becca answer. It's the truckers.

"There are cops all around here," one of them says. "They're going to pick us up. We can't get away. The detonator's set. We're goners."

I look at my watch. It's close to 9:15. We have an hour. At 10:15 either we'll all be dead or we'll have saved the city from destruction. I feel one of those cold shudders pass through my body. I suppose I've lived a sheltered life, but I've never been in a situation where there was a good chance I might die. Sure, the VP's men took a shot at me, but it happened so fast I didn't have a chance to react until it was over. As I recall I did get a little shaky then.

"OK," says Becca. She doesn't say "good luck" or anything. They know if the cops pick the two guys up and hold them, they'll probably be blown to bits. They didn't want it to be a suicide mission, but it might turn out to be one.

"Stay off the phone now," she orders. "I think someone's listening to us."

"Sure." I hear the phones click and realize I probably won't be getting much more information from it.

"I think she's onto us," I say to the trooper.

"It's not surprising. She could see we were anticipating them."

I put the cell phone back in my pocket.

Up ahead I suddenly see the yellowish container. It's

235

slowing, and there are half a dozen police cars all around it, lights flashing, sirens winding down. The truck comes to a stop. The police cars also stop, doors open, and officers come out and crouch behind the doors. We drive up next to one of the police cars. The trooper unhooks a microphone from his dash and flicks a button.

"Come out of the truck slowly with your hands showing!" The words are so loud, they're almost deafening. The truck's door on the driver's side opens, and a leg emerges. I can't see the other side from where I am. A head comes out and looks back. Then the two hands, elevated, empty I'm glad to see. He uses them to grab the handholds and climb down. He seems to be unarmed.

"Lie down, face down, with your hands behind your head!" the lieutenant orders over the loudspeaker. The driver complies. I'm hoping the other trucker also comes out. I look over at the cop to the right of us. He's pointing his gun up a little. I imagine the other trucker's also emerging. I hear helicopter rotors chopping the air in the distance. My heart's pounding at about the same frequency.

The two cops in the car on our left come from behind their open doors and walk slowly toward the trucker, their weapons held two-handedly and trained right at him. He doesn't move. One of the cops reaches down and snaps a handcuff around one wrist then holsters his gun and uses both hands to bring the trucker's arms down to his back and snap the other handcuff in place. Using the handcuffs he hauls the guy to his feet. I get a good look at his face for the first time. It's Yusef. The cops take him back to their car and slide him into the back seat then lock him in there. He looks pale, sort of a gray color.

The other trucker comes around the corner of the truck, his hands behind his back, led by the two cops from the car on our right. I see all the other cops relax and holster their guns. Soon both guys are locked in police cars. The cops have put their guns away, but they still look tense. Why shouldn't they, I think, with that bomb ticking away in there.

Off to the left, a little movement and some color catch my attention. There's a little grassy park and a playground with a set of swings. On one of the swings, a little girl — she can't be more than five years old — is swinging back and forth. She's wearing a red overcoat, and when she swings down, the edges of her coat catch the wind and flip up a little, baring her knees. She watches but doesn't care that a herd of police cars has pulled a truck over. The red coat flaps, and the girl swings innocently. Just off to the right, a bomb is ticking.

The helicopter lands in a parking lot used by the docks. Three people come out, ducking instinctively under the whirling blades even though the blades are ten feet above them. They're all wearing jeans and windbreakers. The windbreakers have something written on them, but they're fluttering so wildly in the downdraft that I can't make it out. Each of them carries a bright-red gym bag as they walk briskly toward us. Two men are in front. Behind them walks a woman, dressed the same way, carrying the same gym bag. They don't run. I want them to hurry. Maybe they don't understand how little time there is. Maybe they want everyone watching to know they're confident. I'm not confident at all. I know they've never tried to disarm an atomic bomb before. I hope it's at least been part of their training.

I get out of the squad car and walk toward the cab of the truck, getting there just a little before the bomb-squad guys. I climb up, open the door, and look in the cab. On the seat is a small, box-shaped device, about nine inches square. The first thing I see are the red digital numbers. They say 60:00:00.

Sixty minutes. That's how much time we have. It doesn't seem like enough to me. A hand comes down on my shoulder, and I jump as if someone's touched me with a cattle prod.

"Let me in, please. Bomb squad." He's calm — businesslike. As I start to back out of the door, the door on the other side opens, and the woman's face appears. She looks serious and businesslike — short-cut, brown hair, blue eyes, and a nice face. She looks like someone I'd like to know, under different circumstances. The thought crosses my mind that I might never get the chance to know her — or anyone else.

I step back and work my way around the guy so he can get in. For the few seconds we share the little steps, our shoulders and hips rub together as I climb down and he climbs up. His body's hard as a rock. Solid bone and flexed muscle — very intense, I think, probably a good thing in a guy who's going to disarm an atomic bomb. As I climb down, I hear the first part of their conversation.

"It's Russian made, see the Cyrillic characters there."

"Right. Pretty standard."

"Yeah," the woman's voice says. "Standard but hard as hell."

"You bet. Probably boobied."

"We should figure on it."

"Turn it over, so we can see the back."

"Well, look at that."

"That's interesting."

After that there is silence, and I climb down to the ground so I'm out of earshot anyway. It sounds as though they know what they're doing. Anyone who can mention how "interesting" a ticking atomic bomb is, has the right academic attitude. The man who'd climbed past me sticks his head out and calls out.

"Is Kimmie Hansen here?"

I raise my hand. "That's me."

"Could you come back up for a minute?"

"Sure." I climb the little ladder again until my head is level with the window. He's sitting on the seat behind the wheel. The timer is between them, where I can't see it. The woman is examining it closely.

"Can you tell me anything about the bomb in the back?"

"Yes. It's an atomic bomb, of the kind they call Little Boy. There's some dynamite or some other regular explosive at one end. The timer sets that off, and it propels something — I'm not sure what — through a barrel to the other end, where the uranium is. That causes the nuclear reaction."

"OK, I know the type. Thanks."

I'm amazed at how casual they are. Then he calls down to one of the guys on the ground.

"We need to set up as wide a perimeter as possible and keep the public out. Contact local law enforcement." Then to his partner, "We should try to sever the connection between the starter and the uranium." I don't hear her answer, but I think she must have said something to the third man, who's on the ground on her side because he runs back to the helicopter at that point.

A guy wearing an NYPD jacket comes up to me. "They tell me you have a cell phone that picks up the perps. Is it still working?"

"Yes, the phone is, but I think they know we're listening in."

"Are you OK in a helicopter?"

"Sure," I lie. I hate them.

"Come with me."

We run back to the helicopter, where we find the third bomb-squad guy unloading a big box.

"D'you have all your stuff out of here?" the cop says. "I need the chopper."

"I'll just get a couple of other things then," the guy says as he hauls two other suitcase-sized objects out of the freight well and puts them on the ground before sliding the door shut.

"It's all yours."

We climb in.

I look back at the scene. Tom's helping the bomb-squad guys open the back of the container. I hate to leave him. I know it's possible I'll never see him again. But it's better to let him help them. He's a good man, I think, and tears well up. My eyes usually behave better. But this is different.

Becca 9:20 a.m.

The helicopter lurches into the air and spins on its axis as soon as the tail clears the trees and electrical wires, which aren't far off. My stomach lurches in reverse, trying to stay on the ground and facing the same direction. I'm not used to the kinds of movements a helicopter makes. I stifle my nausea and look out front, in the direction we're headed, pretending I'm just in a car driving down the highway. It doesn't really work. About every five seconds, something reminds me I'm not in a car but hurtling through the air held up by something like an eggbeater. I keep my hand on my cell phone so I'll be sure to feel it vibrate if a call comes through.

The pilot motions for me to put on the headphones that hang on a hook in front of me. When I do, I can hear him.

"What kind of boat is this couple on?"

"There are two boats. The guy's in one on the East River. He was by the UN, but he's going to continue north, through Hell's Gate and into Long Island Sound. Then he'll head for shore in Connecticut and grab a car."

"And the woman?"

"She's on the Hudson, heading south, to get behind Staten

Island. Maybe farther."

"What kind of boats are they in?"

"I don't know, but they wanted to get fast boats."

"She'd be the only person in the boat?"

"As far as I know."

He fiddles with some dials, and I hear him calling the coast guard. When they answer, he identifies himself and describes the boat and its course and approximate location then offers his assistance in tracking the woman down. I hear him repeat coordinates, probably the area he should patrol. After that the helicopter makes a sharp turn toward the south. I concentrate on not throwing up. By now we're closer to Manhattan than New Jersey, and I'm looking down. If Becca had been at a pier in the area of the 70s, where they'd hoped the truck would end up, she'd be speeding along a line that runs from that position directly to the Narrows. I say this to the pilot, but he just nods. I think he's already figured it all out. Or the coast guard guy told him. We seem to be heading in the right direction.

I start looking. There aren't many small boats on the river, since it's late fall, and of those, not many going fast and heading south, so it's easy to pick her out. She's in an open boat — it must be freezing — going rapidly and heading south. From our height it doesn't seem to be moving fast, but I can see white bow waves thrown to the side as the boat crashes down. We go down to get a closer look, and I can see it's a woman, although I can't really tell if it's Becca. But who else can it be? We keep inching closer. She lets go of the wheel and reaches into a bag and pulls out a gun, turns, and points it at us. The pilot sees what she's doing and jerks the helicopter to one side then leans it forward for speed. My stomach moves more slowly than the chopper. She has to swing around to fire off a shot, and I see muzzle flashes but hear nothing.

There's so much noise; it's impossible to tell if the bullets have gotten close to us. I look at the pilot. He's looking closely at his instruments. He nods and gives me a thumbs-up. No vital parts have been hit. We slew around and climb. I look over at the boat, now off to one side and a little farther away.

She's put the gun down and is steering the boat. I guess when she took her hands off the wheel the boat strayed off course. The boat must have been bouncing too much for her to shoot effectively.

The pilot's talking to the coast guard again, and I hear him give some numbers. We're climbing and heading back in Becca's direction. I see her reach for the gun again, but she seems to think better of the idea and sets it back down. She's probably too far away to shoot at us. We keep climbing and heading toward her until we're directly over her. Then I understand. It's a very awkward place for her to shoot at us, straight overhead, and being there, we broadcast her location to any law enforcement boats in the area. I feel for the first time we're on top of the situation, at least this part of it.

"Where's the coast guard?" It seems to me they should have been here by now.

"I don't know. But they know where we are, and they're on their way."

I keep looking around, but I don't see them. Meanwhile we're approaching the Narrows, and we climb even higher so we can go over the Verrazano Bridge. I'm grateful for that. I don't want to go under it. I can see the boat getting smaller and smaller. Eventually I can't pick it out from the half dozen or so below, going through the strait, all bunched up close to each other because the channel's so narrow.

Once we're over the bridge, we go down again, and fast, which I don't like at all. But in a few seconds, I can pick Becca out. Once she's cleared the Narrows, she starts angling west to get to the other side of Staten Island. We stay right over her.

I look at my watch. It's 9:30. We have 45 minutes before the bomb goes off, unless the bomb-squad guys manage to disarm it.

Then I see the coast guard cutter, moving fast through the water, coming from the east and heading right for Becca. We're directly over her, and that makes it easy for them to locate her. I see them alter course a little to the south. They must have spotted her boat and are putting themselves on a collision course. We stay overhead, but we drop down a little. I can guess why. In just a few minutes, Becca'll have to deal with the approaching coast guard cutter and won't see us as any kind of threat. I'm glad I'm getting a good view. And even gladder to be getting farther away from the activities in Weehawken. The cutter's still quite some distance away when I see a little puff of smoke drifting away from it. I look over at Becca and see the splash in front of her and very close. She swerves, maybe to avoid waves from the splash or just instinctively. She picks up the gun, but the cutter's too far away for her to shoot at. She puts the gun down and swerves toward Staten Island. The cutter alters course slightly. It's becoming less of a convergence and more of a chase.

Fast as she is, the cutter's a little faster, and the distance between them slowly gets smaller and smaller. Nevertheless she's getting closer to the shore, and it looks to me as though she'll get to a pier on Staten Island before the cutter can reach her. I don't think they'll fire at her. There are too many civilians on the land. A miss could be disastrous.

We stay right over her, dropping down even farther, and I can see there are a lot of police cars converging on the area where she'll reach the shore. Apparently she sees them too and heads south. I see some muzzle flashes. Some of the police are firing at her boat. But she has the advantage of being on the water and can go in a straight line. The police cars have to stay on the roads. It looks now as though she might get away.

The coast guard cutter, however, is moving closer and closer. Becca takes a few shots at it but mostly focuses on steering. The cutter turns and runs along parallel to her. The police on the shore seem out of the fight. The cutter keeps edging closer. She takes a couple more shots, but she can't do much. There are a lot of other boats close to the shore that she has to maneuver around. I see ahead of her there's a swampy area where there are no docks and no roads. She's going to ground her boat and run for it. The cutter begins to move in very close. As soon as the area behind her is clear, they fire a shell. It misses but not by much. Then just as she drives her boat into the swamp, a shell hits the boat and explodes. She can't have survived.

We drop down closer. The boat's on fire. No sign of Becca. The cutter comes within a few yards of the shore, and they lower a Zodiac with half a dozen guys in it, all of them armed. I can see the barrels of their guns sticking up in the air, some of them pointing, it seems, at us. I hope they have their safeties on.

There's no movement in the grass or anywhere. We get lower and lower. Then I hear the pilot's voice.

"There's a body lying in the grass, southwest of the boat."

I see her. There's smoke coming from the body, so I figure that was it for Becca. The coast guard Zodiac heads toward her, and the guys get out of the boat and crouch low then advance toward the body.

"No movement," the pilot says. Then the coast guardsmen reach the body and stand around it in a circle. They start to look for weapons and find Becca's blue gym bag.

It's 9:47. I was distracted by the chase, but now I start to tremble again.

Nat 9:50 a.m.

The helicopter rises quickly and spins on its axis, heading

northeast. I grit my teeth against the tilt-a-whirl motion. We're heading for the Hell Gate area, trying to intercept Nat. As soon as the helicopter motion settles down, I call Tom on the cell phone.

"Where are you?"

"I'm still at the Weehawken docks."

"How's the bomb squad doing? Did they defuse the detonator?"

"I thought you knew. You were up there in the cab." He sounds very calm.

"Knew what?" I shout in exasperation.

"The drivers never set the detonator. It was turned on, but the last button hadn't been pushed, and the timer wasn't running."

I remember then that when I looked at the box on the front seat of the cab, the red letters had said "60:00:00." If it'd been running, they'd have said something less than that, and the 100^{ths} would have been moving. Relief runs through my body like a warm fluid, and I think for a minute I'm going to pee in my pants. It's over. The danger's past. I swear to myself a little and then think about Tom.

"Have the bomb-squad guys left?"

"No. They've opened up the container and thrown out a lot of stuff that was in there just to cover up the bomb. They have an acetylene torch inside the container, and they're cutting the barrel part in half to separate the two nuclear parts. They've managed to clear the area too."

"Just taking no chances?"

"Right. Considering the potential for damage, it seems the prudent thing to do."

I agree with him on that, and I'm glad to hear they're cutting through the barrel.

"They're making progress on cutting the barrel. No, wait, they've stopped cutting."

I hear him shout, "What's the problem?"

There's a silence while someone gives him a brief report.

"Oh, damn," I hear him say.

"What's the matter?"

"The barrel got too hot. They were afraid the heat would detonate the conventional explosive, so they've called for a pumper to come and douse that end with water, but it hasn't come yet."

But as soon as he tells me this, he says the pumper's arrived. I can hear the relief in his voice.

"They're running a fire hose from the river up to the container. OK. I think they're cutting the barrel again while they run water over the end where the charge is. Jesus!"

"What?" I'm afraid I've missed something; it's hard to understand with the noise of the helicopter rotors in the background.

"Nothing. It's just close. Too close. Nobody knows how much heat it'll take to set off the dynamite. They're bringing a bomb truck up now."

I know what he means by a bomb truck. One of those reinforced trucks you can put an explosive inside. But it'll be useful only if they can cut through the barrel and separate the regular charge from the nuclear one. The bomb truck would never contain a nuclear explosion.

The helicopter lurches again as we change course for some reason. We're crossing over the northern tip of Manhattan. I look down and see the Cloisters, green squares, outlined by cream-colored and gray buildings. I've spent some happy hours there, and even from this height, I sense the serenity of that place. It contrasts with the urgency that's driving us toward

Connecticut. Around the Cloisters I can see the streets of northern Manhattan — Dykeman St. crossing the island, and in the north the playing fields of Columbia. I can imagine the bustling life going on down there — merchants selling wares, people shopping, kids playing in the parks, and inside the apartments, people making love, chatting about the weather, reading the latest novels, watching TV. None of them knows how close it's been.

I look over at the pilot. He seems very sure of himself, and I think he really likes flying the helicopter. I realize I'm smiling. It's hard not to smile.

"The bomb's not going to go off," I say to him over the intercom.

"I know. The drivers never set the detonator."

"You knew? Why didn't you say something?"

"I thought you knew. You were up there in the truck."

"But I didn't know it hadn't been set. I heard the drivers telling Becca they were going to set it."

"They lied."

"Jesus!" I shout. I could have been spared at least 30 minutes of excruciating anxiety. For a few minutes, I'm really pissed and want to hit somebody. Then just as fast as my temper flared, I calm down. What's over is over. Of course, realizing you're going to survive when you thought you might not improves your frame of mind.

We come out over Long Island Sound. It's narrow at first, but as we fly along heading east it gets wider and wider. We start looking down. If Nat was down by the UN at 8:30 when he was talking to Becca, he should be in the Sound by now. It's almost 9:55. He'll be expecting the bomb to go off any minute, probably already wondering why it hasn't. But he wasn't in on the conversation Becca had with the drivers, so he has only a vague idea of when it might have been set. I wonder what would have happened to us if it had gone off as planned. We were about 15 miles from Weehawken, I think, but we were up in the air, without any protection. The pilot's voice sounds in my ear, breaking off my speculation.

"There he is!"

I look down and see a lone man in a speedboat going fast, headed east. We go down for a closer look. I see the man look up, and I can tell it's Nat. Next to him on the seat is a blue bag just like the one Becca had. Hers had a gun in it.

"He's probably armed!" I shout into my mouthpiece. The pilot nods and immediately pulls back on the stick. We jerk upwards. Nat was reaching for the blue bag, but when we jerked upward, I lost sight of him, so I can't tell if he's taken a gun out of it. And I know I won't hear the bullets if there are any. Nothing happens.

I check my watch again. 10:01. I call Tom.

"Hi," he answers, "I'm glad you called."

"How's it going?"

"They've separated the nuclear part from the dynamite, and they're transferring the dynamite to the truck. It looks like they're going to get it contained."

"I love you." I'm surprised to hear those words come out of my mouth. I've never said them to anyone before, and I've been around for a long time.

"I love you too. And we're going to be together," he adds in a husky voice.

Relief and other feelings I can't describe flood over me. I'm not going to die in a fireball in the middle of the air over Long Island Sound. I'm going to feel Tom's arms around me again. We're going to snuggle down under the covers, naked, and make love. I realize I'm totally turned on. I've never felt so sexual.

The pilot's talking into his microphone, saying numbers, and I know he's talking to the coast guard. I give him the thumbs-up sign. He stops talking for a minute. His eyebrows are up.

"No explosion. They took care of the bomb."

He looks at his watch and smiles, giving me a thumbs-up sign back. Then he starts talking to the coast guard again. The guy's a real pro.

I look out the window just as Nat's boat makes a sharp left turn. We turn again, maintaining a position over the boat so the coast guard can find Nat. I look around, and then I see him, coming very fast from the west. Nat's still going fast, bouncing over the waves, heading for the Connecticut shore, which isn't very far away. He's going to make it too, I realize. Maybe he still thinks the bomb's going to go off.

I can see where he's heading — a marina filled with sailboats and motorboats, next to the Connecticut Turnpike. I've seen this same marina many times as I've driven over the bridge and looked down. It's just over the Connecticut state line. The pilot switches the frequency of his radio, and I hear him talking again; this time, I assume, to the Connecticut state police. I watch Nat come up to a dock, grab his blue gym bag, and jump out of the boat, just letting it drift. Why would he bother tying it up? He runs up the dock and into the parking lot.

"He's going to steal a car," I shout to the pilot as I see a white SUV pull into the lot. Poor guy, I think; he has no clue. Nat has his gun out, and I can imagine that down on the dock and in the parking lot, people are screaming, but from up here it's all just the sound of our motor. I see the driver of the SUV tumble out of the door, his hands up, and run across the lot, finding a place to hide behind another car. Nat jumps into the SUV, makes a fast U-turn, and heads out of the parking lot.

We can see him plainly, and I hear the pilot describing the car to the state police dispatcher. I watch the car leave the parking lot, accelerate along a small access road, and then go up a ramp to the Turnpike. It doesn't look like he's going very fast from where I am, but he's passing all the other cars on the Turnpike, and that's saying something.

***

We keep our position steadily over the speeding car. Nat knows by now something's gone wrong, at least a bad delay. Soon he'll realize the bomb's not going to go off at all, and because he's being pursued, he knows the plot's been discovered. I wonder what he's thinking. Probably just get away, lose the cops, and find a place where he can ditch the car and disappear. I wonder if he knows anything about the area. Probably not, since he grew up in Iowa. I certainly know the area. We're getting closer and closer to Darien, where I grew up. All those cops down there know the area too, probably better than I do.

Occasionally the pilot answers something from the police with a single word. I can't hear the police side of the conversation, but it's obvious the pilot's helping them coordinate some plan that'll help them stop the speeding car. Now a half dozen or more police cars are chasing the white SUV. Nat's driving very fast, changing lanes rapidly as he passes cars. It's a situation where somebody could be hurt, and I know the cops want to end it as soon as they can.

I look ahead and see traffic's slowing down and stopping. They must have put up a roadblock, but it must be a mile or two down the road, and now several thousand cars are stopped between the SUV and the roadblock. It looks as though they made a stupid mistake. He might try to go across the median and go in the opposite direction. On the right side of the road, there's an exit. It's an exit I know well from when I was a little girl — Rowayton, a small area near Darien. There's a road leading down to the water. He's pulling to the right. He almost misses the exit, but at the last minute he swerves and runs down the little hill toward the road that leads to the water. He's either going to get mired down in little streets or get lost in them and escape.

As Nat gets to the foot of the ramp, three police cars pull suddenly across in front of him. They've been waiting behind bushes off to the side. I didn't even see them myself. He aims for the space between two of them and tries to crash through with his heavier vehicle. The two police cars part like the doors of a gate, but they're scraping along the sides of his car, and he can't go fast. I see muzzle flashes from police guns on both sides of the roadblock. The SUV's through the roadblock, but the driver's door opens, and Nat falls out and lies on the ground.

Troopers and local police run up to him. They have him. I can't tell if he's hurt or not. We're low enough that I can see them putting handcuffs on him, so he's alive.

An ambulance comes roaring up, braking hard. I can see the smoke where the tires skid on the pavement. It's eerie to watch and not hear any sound. The ambulance probably had its siren going full blast too, but I hear only the helicopter motor.

The attendants jump out and follow the policemen's waving arms toward the two police cars Nat crashed through. Maybe the guys in those vehicles were hurt. Both cops emerge at the same time from the passenger doors of their cars. They're walking, but the EMS guys help them into the ambulance. They must have rattled around inside their vehicles when the SUV knocked them off to the side. Then the EMS guys go to Nat, who's still lying on his stomach, with his hands cuffed behind his back. The police back off to let them through. I'll bet they're reluctant to give Nat much medical help. I've covered more than one police chase, and when they catch the guy, they're never too happy with him.

The EMS technicians roll Nat on his side. A conversation's going on. Probably they're asking him where it hurts or can he wiggle his toes. After a bit they help him to his feet and steer him toward the ambulance. He goes in with the two cops from the cars, and two other officers follow him into the back of the ambulance. Then it pulls away. I can find out later what hospital they're taking him to because I want to talk to him. I want an interview, but I know it'll be difficult to get now that he's in police custody.

So, I think, we have four of them. Al and Muhammad are still not accounted for. I call Tom.

"Hi." There's a cheerfulness in his voice I haven't heard for a while. "It's good to hear from you."

"Sounds like you might be having a little party over there."

"Yeah, we're pretty happy around here. The dynamite went off inside the bomb truck like it was supposed to, and they've unloaded the nuclear charge from the container. They've called for another vehicle to take that away after they make sure it's safe. We're just wrapping things up, talking to each other, getting our reports straight. Where are you?"

"They've caught Nat. Outstanding police work here; he's in custody going to a hospital. I don't know anything about his injuries, but he seemed to be walking OK."

"Why don't you come over here?"

"I'll do that." I feel things happening in my chest, good things, like champagne bubbles and falling confetti.

"Can we go back to Weehawken?" I ask the pilot.

"Sure. It's all over here, for sure." The chopper turns and lifts, and we head southwest. I watch out the window as we fly over Westchester County. I recognize some of the highways. Off to the right, I can see parts of White Plains, and then we're over the river. To the north the new Tappan Zee Bridge looks beautiful. I never realized how beautiful a bridge could be. It curves around and up and down in the most graceful way. Of course it's my brain that's feeling beautiful and graceful at that moment. I suppose if I'd stepped in dogshit I'd have said, "Isn't that interesting how soft and pungent it is?" Life is just perfect at this moment.

We come down in the same Weehawken docks parking lot. The container truck's still there with its now famous red cowling. I see a photojournalist taking a picture of it as we settle down to the ground. A little bump and we're there. I unbuckle myself, kiss the pilot on the cheek, get out and duck low as I scramble away from the chopper and up toward the container truck. There are now thousands of people around. Onlookers have appeared out of nowhere, and there are journalists, several TV broadcasting trucks, way more cops, and quite a few officials. If he isn't there already, I'm sure the mayor of New York City will be there soon. Probably the mayor of Weehawken is already there, but no one would recognize him. Soon he'll have his picture in a lot of newspapers.

I work my way through the crowd toward the container truck. A line of police tape keeps the crowd back about 30 feet. I see him, standing next to the truck talking to someone in civilian clothes.

"Tom!" I yell as loud as I can to get over the noise. He hears my voice and turns. I duck under the tape and run to him. He comes toward me in that purposeful stride he has that I must have always loved but never thought about before. He kisses me and holds me tightly.

"We're going to be OK." He can hardly talk, but he says all

the right things.

"I know." I throw my arms around his neck and hold my face up to be kissed. He doesn't disappoint me.

We're still deep in liplock when my phone buzzes. It's Gaylord.

"What kind of trick you playing on Gaylord, Kimmie?"

"Are you in Poughkeepsie?"

"Yes, I'm in Poughkeepsie, but where are you? Where are all the signs you said would be here? I thought we were going to have a party. I even bought a new outfit, and I want you to see it."

"I'm sorry, Gaylord. I had to get you out of New York. There were… No, I can't tell you over the phone. Come back to New York. We have some celebrating to do."

"Kimmie darling, I never thought of you as mysterious. This new persona is something I find very interesting."

"So come on back down here to real life, and I'll tell you tales to straighten your hair."

"Well it's been getting a little too tight in the curl lately. I'll be glad to come back. Poughkeepsie isn't my cup of tea, if you know what I mean. Did you know there are Vassar girls everywhere, and not only that, there are Vassar men here now too? They all look very cute to me, but I'll drag myself away on the promise of a party."

"Good. Call me when you get in. We have a lot to talk about."

Then I call Col. Haldane. She picks up the phone herself.

"Hi, Kimmie. I've been watching the news. Everything looks good."

"Everything's just fine." I squeeze Tom's shoulder with my free hand. "I'm here with Tom."

"Mmmhmm, I'm getting the picture." I can hear the smile

in her voice. "I'll be in New York tomorrow. Maybe you'll introduce me."

"I'd like that. Maybe I can interview you for another story?"

We make arrangements. I'm looking forward to introducing these two people I admire so much. But I'm going to make sure Tom stays close to me. I'm not taking any chances on this big Roxie girl.

Cargo

EPILOGUE

Waziristan

Golutsov no longer wears Western clothes. Instead he dresses in long, white Arab robes, with a checkered scarf tied with a cord around his forehead. His sandals make a sound like small waves striking wet sand as he walks across the carpet toward the New Leader, who sits in the same chair he was in before, surrounded by several massive guards, the richness of Persian carpet and thick, woven wall hangings. In front of the New Leader is a small table with fruit and a plate of sweets, a samovar, and two teacups. A chair has been placed on the other side of it. He smiles at the New Leader with a clear sense of accomplishment and extends his hand as he approaches, but the New Leader gestures with his right hand for him to sit down in the chair that has been placed in front of him. The smile vanishes.

"*Effendi*," he says, his voice trembling a little. "Is there news?"

"Yes, there is news."

"And our Little Boy? Has he done his mischief?"

"He has not. The attempt has failed."

"Oh, this is a great pity," the man says, sitting back in the chair heavily, his body sagging.

"Yes," says the New Leader evenly. "It is a great pity."

"Your men there. Are they all right?" the man asks.

"The woman is dead. The police are holding the two drivers. I do not know yet about the other three."

Golutsov shakes his head in a mixture of disbelief, sorrow, and apology. Then he stops and begins to say something to the

New Leader, but as he does so, one of the huge guards walks behind him silently, crosses his hands, and quickly slips a wire over his head. Then he pulls his hands apart, pulling the garrote so tight that blood oozes out in a ring around the man's neck. Red drops fall and stain the white robes he is wearing. Golutsov reaches up to his neck to get his fingers under the wire, but he cannot even find the wire. It has sunk into his flesh. His eyes bulge, and his tongue protrudes in a desperate attempt at air. His legs kick out helplessly. The guard transfers the handle of the garrote that has been in his left hand to his right, so that both handles are in one hand, then using both hands, he twists the wire quickly several times so that the pressure is maintained. He turns casually, holding the two handles in one hand, and walks toward the door. The chair that Golutsov sat in tips over backward, and he falls to the floor. He tries to get his feet under his body, but the huge guard walks slowly and easily toward the door, dragging the man behind him with little difficulty. He might be walking through an airport with wheeled luggage for all the concern he shows. The guards standing by the door open it so the man dragging the garroted victim can pass through. Golutsov's kicking is already subsiding into twitches. As he is dragged out of the chamber, his hands fall to his sides and drag on the floor, and his knees bend spasmodically. The door closes behind him with a thud. He is now a dead weight dragged by the heavy guard toward the front of the cave.

When the macabre pair reach the cave entrance, the man is already dead, and the guard who had killed him hitches him forward toward the entrance. He unwinds the twisted wires of the garrote, and with his knee propels the body out of the cave. He lets go of one of the garotte handles and holds the other as he shoves the body out. The man's body twists once in the air before falling down the mountainside, creating a cloud of dust and a shower of small stones.

The guard retains the garrote. He turns and walks back into the cave.

Nina is not sure how she feels.

ACKNOWLEDGMENTS

My first thanks are to my father, who punished me for some unremembered misdeed by making me write an essay on what I did wrong and why it was wrong to do it. I have no memory of what it was I did, or why, but I remember enjoying the process of finding the right words and making them fit together.

I remember with gratitude a few of the teachers who helped to improve my writing with generous criticism — Al Olsen, George Gurney, Jascha Kessler. Then a few who inspired me through their own writing — Charles Van Riper, Lewis Thomas, E.O. Wilson, Patrick O'Brian.

As always, I am grateful to my wife, Janet Givens, for just about everything — love, criticism, support, focus, and companionship.

Woody Starkweather
In the Vermont woods,
in a deepening spring snowfall, 2019

ABOUT THE AUTHOR

Woody Starkweather has been a life-long lover of words: spoken, written, or sung. After a long career helping those who struggle with speech, he and his wife, Janet Givens, joined the Peace Corps and taught English in Central Asia. Now they write —she memoirs, he novels— amid the Vermont woods

www.ingramcontent.com/pod-product-compliance
Lightning Source LLC
Chambersburg PA
CBHW020554180626
46810CB00007B/2507